ALL SUMMER THROUGH

MALCOLM SAVILLE

All Summer Through

Illustrated by Joan Kiddell-Monroe

BROCKHAMPTON PRESS

Published by Brockhampton Press Ltd
Market Place, Leicester
Printed in Great Britain
by Richard Clay and Company Ltd
Bungay, Suffolk 63.4

CONTENTS

1

THE WISE OWL

THE three Richardson children lived in an old house over their father's bookshop, the *Wise Owl*, in the main street of a country town called Nettleford.

Let's be introduced to them early on the first morning of the summer holidays.

Sally, the eldest, is just thirteen. Small, slight and with a head of shining, dark hair and smoky grey eyes like her mother. She has just counted the strokes of the church clock and to her astonishment only made them six.

'Why on earth am I awake at this hour?' she thought as she turned over. 'Am I feeling all right?' After considering this important matter for a few drowsy moments she decided that she was well but felt rather empty inside and that this feeling was not due to hunger.

'I'm excited 'cos there's no school today nor for weeks and weeks. That's what it is, but I can't think why I'm so babyish as to feel like it. I shan't tell Paul. There's days and days stretching ahead almost like eternity' (Sally sometimes thought like this to herself), 'to do things in and to do nothing in – practically all summer in fact, and I have to wake early on the one day that I needn't. I'm wasting good sleeping time.'

She put her hands behind her head and looked at the ceiling through half-closed eyes. That was rather silly because the cracks in the discoloured plaster looked like streams and rivers on a map and reminded her of geography which she hated almost as much as maths . . . How wonderful to have no school . . . No rushing at breakfast . . . No last hunt round for books and satchel and beret . . . No dashing for the bus . . . No more of Miss Turner's sarcastic tongue – 'Perhaps Sally Richardson, who obviously knows so much that she can afford to pay so little attention, will kindly step up here and elucidate this problem for us.' . . . No more school. Lovely! Elizabeth home from boarding school today. Then holidays all together and the seaside with the family in two weeks' time . . .

She closed her eyes and when she woke again the sun had reached her open window. Specks of dust danced lazily in the beam which lit up the faded red roses of the wall-paper above her bed. From below came the sound of the milkman's whistle and the thud as he put down the bottles on the doorstep, and in the distance the faint cawing of the rooks in the elms round the vicarage garden.

She got out of bed. The linoleum was pleasantly cool to her bare feet as she padded over to the open window and leaned out over the sill. It certainly was a glorious morning, for a haze of heat was already hanging over the rooftops. Below her, in the tiny back garden behind the shop, a cat was stalking an unsuspecting blackbird. She shouted a warning and grimaced at the furious tabby and then, because the window-sill hurt her tummy, she slipped back into the room.

'I don't suppose I shall ever wake so early again,' she thought, 'and I *could* start the holidays really well by making them all some tea . . . I'll get Paul up to help.'

Paul was eleven and his room was just across the landing. According to Sally he was noisy, grubby, and bossy, besides being spoiled by his mother, but the truth was that he was just a normal small boy with an engaging smile and a great sense of humour. Sally and he squabbled a good deal but deep down were extremely fond of each other.

She reached for her dressing-gown, banged on his door and walked in. The room looked as if a tornado had passed through it. None of the Richardsons was tidy but Paul's room was a disgrace. He insisted upon having his bed directly under his window so that there was more floor space for the layout of his railway. The top of his chest of drawers was a muddle of half-constructed models, a pile of flints which he hoped one day to chip into the shape of arrow-heads, and some boxes of birds' eggs, most of which had been cracked for some time. On the mantelpiece was a collection of what he called 'Relics'. Sally had frequently told him that he meant 'Souvenirs' and should try to use the right word, but he stuck to 'Relics' although he could not always remember what they all were or where they came from. There was, for instance, a glass tube of coloured sands which he had swopped for something at school, several metal models of farmyard animals which he was going to repaint and give to Veronica one day, the jawbone of a sheep which he had picked up in the country, a bundle of bus tickets and a propelling pencil with an advertisement on its side. Relics came and relics were exchanged for other relics, but the collection as a whole was cherished fanatically and nobody was allowed to touch the mantelpiece.

There was a photograph of the elegant Denis Compton stuck slightly askew on one wall and a lurid print of camels passing in convoy in front of some pyramids, on another.

Paul could never give a reasonable explanation of why he liked this crude picture, except that the sunset looked like a broken egg.

On the chair by his bed was a pile of books but Sally didn't look twice at these for there were books in every room in the Richardson home.

Paul himself was peacefully asleep, half inside the bed-clothes and half out, with an expanse of skin showing between the two portions of his pyjamas. When she called his name he grunted and turned over but kept his eyes closed. His tousled hair – very much lighter than her own or his mother's – seemed to be tickling his forehead for he brushed a hand across his face as he muttered,

'Go 'way, whoever you are, unless it's you, Mum. I'm still asleep.'

Suddenly Sally was reminded of how he looked when he was a very little boy, and indeed he did not look very much older now as he lay there with the sunshine across his freckled nose and his closed eyes. Maybe it wasn't fair to wake him so early, and as she was feeling in such a beautiful mood she would get the tea by herself. She stepped back towards the door and trod on a tin petroleum van belonging to the railway set. It had sharp edges. She was not wearing shoes and as her foot hurt very much she kicked the van out of the way with a clatter. Paul stirred again and turned over with a sigh as she slammed his door and limped downstairs.

The *Wise Owl* was a tall, narrow building, with a big sitting- and dining-room and the kitchen on the first floor, bathroom and two bedrooms on the next and two more rooms and a boxroom at the top. All the rooms had sloping floors and for as long as she could remember – they had lived at the *Wise Owl* for six years – it had been necessary to keep a wad of paper under the table legs so that they shouldn't wobble. It was a fascinating house.

The stairs seemed to creak more than usual as she hobbled down to the kitchen and lit the gas under 'Goldie'. All the kettles in the Richardson family were named and this one, the favourite, had been so christened by Veronica because it was made of copper. For a moment Sally wondered whether she would wake her six-year-old sister and then decided that she would probably wake as soon as she heard someone talking in her mother's room. She clattered three cups on a tray and then ran back to the bathroom. Her tooth-paste was under the bath, which was not where she had left it, and paste was oozing from the wrong end of the tube which had a dent in the middle. She knew the culprit and gritted her teeth at the thought of what she would say to Paul at breakfast.

Goldie was boiling furiously by the time she had dressed and she was feeling rather pleased with herself when she put the tray down on the floor outside her parents' room and tapped the brass knocker on the door.

'It's seven o'clock, Mummy. May I come in? I've got a surprise.'

Sally loved this room. She had loved it from the day her mother had first taken her into her own bed to comfort her when she was not well, until now when she was beginning to be grown-up and could sit on the end of it and chat, woman to woman. She loved the muddle on the dressing-table, the smell of spilled powder and the feel of the white hairbrush with a silver 'M' on the back, against her own sleek head. She loved her father's corner and the muddle from his pockets on his table and the smell of tobacco hanging about the clothes in his wardrobe.

'Come in, darling,' a sleepy voice called. 'What's happened to get you up so early?'

Sally turned the handle, picked up the tray and banged the door shut with her behind.

'A surprise. I've made you some tea. Good morning, Mummy. Good morning, Pops. It's time you were moving.'

Margaret Richardson was ten years younger than her husband and as she sat up and reached for her dressing-jacket she did not look much older than Sally, and very like her. She had the same short, glistening, black hair with a slight wave in it, and the same wide, grey eyes. Nobody would have guessed this morning that she was the mother of three children and the mainspring of the Richardson family. Almost everything that happened to the Richardsons was due to her. Even the *Wise Owl* had been her idea.

As Sally turned from the window her father ran a hand through the few hairs which were left on the top of his head and reached for his spectacles.

'Did I hear you call me "Pops", Sally?'

'Yes, Daddy, but I've brought you some tea.'

'I am impervious to bribes and I will not be called "Pops" by any of you. I wish you would train your children, Margaret. They have no respect for their aged parents . . . Please don't fiddle with that table, Sally. What do you want?'

'I want to put the tray down somewhere and kiss you "Good morning". I do think you might say that you're glad to see me, Daddy.'

'Nearly always glad,' he smiled as he adjusted his spectacles and sat up. 'No . . . Wait. I'll move those books and papers. You'll muddle them.'

It was hardly possible for them to be in a greater muddle than they were already but Mr Richardson hated anyone but himself touching his books and all that he did now was to sweep the pile on to the floor between the beds with a grand gesture.

'There you are, child. How many spoonfuls did you put in the pot? Two and a half? Good. You'll be a better tea maker than your mother yet . . . Pour it out and give her the first cup and leave the stronger one for me.'

Sally poured the tea and, balancing her own cup carefully, climbed to the end of her mother's bed.

'Are you pleased with me, Mummy? If you like I'll get the breakfast – although I shall jolly well make Paul help me this time,' she added in an undertone.

'It's wonderful service, darling, and of course we're pleased . . . Couldn't you sleep?'

There was a twinkle in her eye that checked Sally's indignation.

'Not very well,' she admitted. 'I woke at six feeling excited inside, like I did when I was quite young. I think it's 'cos it's the first day of the holidays. Do you think we could do something special?'

'We might,' Margaret admitted, 'but there's the raspberry jam to make. Wilfred darling! Let's do something all together this afternoon? It's Wednesday. Half-day.'

Her husband put his cup down on the floor.

'I can never really get away from any of you . . . But I'll tell you what I will do. For seven months now old Mrs

Battersby has owed me nine pounds. Not only has she bought books for which she has not paid but she comes back again and again to the shop and reads off the shelves for nothing . . . If her cheque has arrived this morning we will go out somewhere and celebrate . . . Now run away, Sally, and see if there's a letter in the post that looks as if it has a cheque in it . . . I want to get up.'

Before she could answer, a crash on the door announced the arrival of Paul. He stood just inside the room with his hair all over the place and a grin on his face as he clutched his pyjama trousers with one hand and pointed accusingly at Sally with the other.

'Listen, Mum,' he began. 'Why do you let her make such a row in the morning? She's been crashing up and down stairs and banging my door and upsetting my room for half an hour . . . What are you all talking about, anyway?' he added suspiciously.

'You lazy, noisy brat,' Sally began, 'I believe you were awake all the time. And you might say you're sorry now for interrupting us.'

'Don't be silly, Sally,' her mother said, 'and don't start squabbling now . . . We weren't talking about anything special, Paul. Only wondering what we were going to do this afternoon as Daddy will be with us and it's the first day of the holidays.'

'I'm going fishing,' Paul said with another heave at his pyjamas. 'I fixed it yesterday.'

'We're talking about doing something *together*,' Sally explained carefully, but feeling very angry.

Paul grinned impudently.

'I don't mind any of you coming with me if you keep

quiet. I arranged to go with Jimmy but you don't have to come if you don't want to, Sall . . . May I have some tea, please? I'm jolly thirsty. I s'pose it's all this talking so early in the morning.'

'You can take the tray and help yourself in the kitchen,' his father said, 'and I know it won't worry you in the slightest, my boy, but you are not to go into the bathroom until I have finished shaving . . . Now please go away.'

'Just see what's happened to Veronica, Sally,' Margaret said. 'Will you get her up and then start the toast? . . . Thank you for a lovely surprise.'

Veronica was not very much like the others – certainly not as pretty as Sally nor as robust as Paul, and a little spoiled. She was sitting up in bed talking to Hubert, a white teddy-bear without a head, when Sally came in. Like all the Richardsons she loved books but had a passion for being read to and an obstinate preference for a few cherished stories all of which the rest of the family had long since committed to memory.

'Hullo, Sall!' she said. 'I'd like you to read to me before I get up. I'd like you to read about Peter Rabbit squeezin' under the gate of Mr Ergreggor's garden . . . Oh! very well. I didn't really think you would. You're horrid to me. Everyone's unkind to me except dear Hubert here and he's often naughty. What shall I wear?'

Sally started her sister on the road to another day and then ran down to the kitchen where she found Paul looking distastefully at two pairs of dirty shoes.

'Why did you mess up my tooth-paste?' she demanded. 'You squeezed it in the middle and then threw it under the bath.'

Paul was now wearing a dark blue shirt open at the neck, corduroy shorts and sandals, and he smiled at her disarmingly. He never bore malice.

'I was just wondering what I could offer you if you'd clean the family shoes, Sall. I can't think of anything that I hate more. I'm no good at it either. Some things you hate but you know you can do them, but this isn't one of those things. Besides I want to get some worms. Will you help me do Dad's shoes, Sall? I'll give you something if you will.'

'Maybe I'll help you after breakfast,' she said graciously. 'Will you start the toast? I'm going down for the letters.'

He nodded gloomily, put down his father's shoes and lit the gas under the grill.

The *Wise Owl* shop was long and narrow. The shop door was at the side and opened straight on to the pavement, and beside it was the window with white shelves at the back where Wilfred made displays of the new books. Inside it was not at all like an ordinary shop but that, as Margaret always said, 'was the idea'. Shelves stretched from floor to ceiling on each side and these were neatly labelled – 'Cheap Classics', 'History', 'English Literature', 'Poetry', 'Fiction', 'Whodunits', 'Natural History' and in the far corner up by the old table which Wilfred used as a counter was the special corner where the children's books were kept. Behind the table was another little room which was known as 'the office' during business hours and 'the study' at all other times. Behind Wilfred's chair there was an old-fashioned iron stove which belched yellowish fumes when the wind was in the east, and a green-shaded lamp with a little hanging chain to switch it on and off on his roll-top desk. This lamp reminded Sally of their very first

day at the *Wise Owl*, for she had played with it then as her
father stood by helplessly, while Margaret, in a whirlwind
of dust and energy, tried to organize them all into activity.

It was to the study that Wilfred sometimes retired in the evenings and here that Sally had had some of her most wonderful talks with him – talks about books in particular, but sometimes about life in general. The way in which her father often spoke to her as if she was grown-up was one of his greatest gifts, and the two of them had created a very rare companionship because of it. They talked together as friends talk.

Just inside the narrow door at the foot of the stairs leading from the house to the shop was another tiny office with a frosted glass front. This office was not much more than a box and it belonged to 'Phelpy', Wilfred's only assistant.

Miss Phelps knew not only about real books but about book-keeping as well and it was from this little glass-fronted box that the accounts were sent out each month to customers and where – and this was very much more unpleasant – cheques to publishers were made out ready for Wilfred's unwilling signature. The till was here also – a long, narrow contraption with a glass panel in the lid. You wrote with a pencil through a slit in the glass and then pulled out the drawer sharply to put in the money or fumble for change, and when you pulled, the paper on which you had written moved round so that there was a clean space for the next entry. Once the till had been fitted with a little bell which tinged when you pulled the drawer, but Wilfred had removed this because he said it sounded 'too commercial'.

Margaret often told him that he was not commercial enough.

But Sally did not even peep into the office this morning, for she could see the pile of letters on the door-mat. There was always a thrill in looking through the mail. 'There may well be romance or tragedy in every delivery the postman makes,' her father had once told her and she always remembered this as she sorted the letters. She put them into three piles – rather like a game of patience. The first, of private letters for the family, the next of all shapes and sizes which were obviously for the business, and the last all those with twopenny-halfpenny stamps. This last pile was always left in the glass box for Phelpy because Wilfred had once told Sally that bills at breakfast ruined his day.

As she ran upstairs again she heard her mother's voice raised in protest in the kitchen and the smell of burning toast told her without words that Paul was doing his job only too well. Her father was standing by the breakfast table in the living-room and turned with a welcoming smile as she came in.

'How nice he is,' she thought with a sudden warm rush of affection.

Wilfred really only seemed to be tall when standing by his wife, but he was certainly distinguished looking. There was something of the schoolmaster about him when he put on his heavy, horn-rimmed spectacles, and his expression, though sometimes anxious, was always intelligent. He had long, sensitive fingers and kindly blue eyes, and walked with a slight stoop. Nothing that his wife did could make his clothes look tidy and nothing that she said could deter him from wearing a blue bowtie with white spots with every suit he had.

'Here's the post, Daddy. I'm afraid there's a biggish pile for Phelpy downstairs. Please look and see if Mrs Battersby has sent a cheque.'

She had not. The post was what Wilfred called 'dull'.

'Never mind, Sall,' he said, 'we'll have a wonderful beano when it does come just because I've given up all hope of getting it . . . Here are two letters for your mother and one of them is from your Aunt Janet in London. Put them on her plate . . . What are you going to do this morning? I'm expecting some parcels. Perhaps you would like to come down presently and help us unpack them?'

Sally never tired of the thrill of unpacking new books. The parcels were always so beautifully rectangular and so neatly tied. The string snapped back if you were impatient and cut it. The packing-paper inside was often uncut sheets of the pages of other books and then, of course, the actual books themselves smelled of ink and shiny paper, were smooth to touch and exciting to examine.

Before she could answer, Margaret came in with the tray, followed by Veronica clasping two boxes of cornflakes. Paul, with a smudge of blacking on his snub nose, slipped into his place and sat poised for instant action as his father said grace and then unfolded the newspaper with an air that suggested that he already knew the worst.

Margaret believed in making meals into social occasions and conversation was encouraged so long as they didn't all interrupt each other and had something worthwhile to say. Wilfred was often difficult because he preferred a book or a paper, and was never at his best at breakfast anyway, because he was invariably depressed by the news.

This morning was no exception and after Margaret had reminded them that as there was no school there was no need to bolt their food, Veronica, with a moustache of cream on her upper lip, turned to her sister and said brightly:

'Whatever you do and wherever you go today, Sall, I want to do it and go it with you. I'm looking forward to your holiday very much . . . So is Hubert.'

Sally was surprised at this show of affection because Veronica usually preferred her mother's company.

'Did you hear what she said, Mummy?' she began, and then stopped in surprise when she noticed that Margaret, with a piece of toast in one hand and the sheet of a long letter in the other, was not even listening. She was frowning, and when Paul said, 'What's up, Mum? Has anything awful happened?' she shook her head vaguely, and murmuring, 'Just a minute, children,' put down the fourth sheet and turned to the fifth.

'By the appearance of the writing and the length of the letter, I suggest that your sister Janet has written to you,' Wilfred said. 'I hope you have not had bad news?'

'No, darling,' she said doubtfully. 'Not really. I'll give you this to read later and we must talk about it.'

'Can't you tell us, Mummy?' Sally persisted. 'Is it awful?'

'Don't worry me, Sall,' was all she would say, and after that an awkward silence fell on the breakfast table until Veronica spoke loudly.

'I wish people would talk. It's awful when they don't. I'm sorry if something is wrong, but I promise it's nothing to do with me. What are you going to do after breakfast, Sall?'

'She's going to take you out for an hour while I talk to Daddy,' Margaret said. 'Paul has already told us that he wants worms, so he can go off collecting the horrible things just as soon as he's ready . . . Now don't all look so glum. We'll do something together this afternoon, I promise.'

'I'm not really sure about the worms,' Paul said when the door had closed behind the children, 'but I expect I shall. I wonder what that letter is about?'

'I don't know. I wish I did. I'm curious . . . You'd better go and wash your face and then finish doing Dad's shoes, and then you can come and find us if you like. Or are you going to play with your grubby little friend, Jimmy?'

'Shucks!' Paul said as he went back to the kitchen. He had just read this word in a cowboy story and liked it. 'Shucks to you, sister. You think you're grown-up, but you're only stuck-up. I'll clean the shoes and then I'll do what I want and not what you want.'

He slammed the kitchen door and then opened it again. 'You promised to help me with the shoes after breakfast . . . Just like a girl.'

'He's very rude,' Veronica said primly as she took her sister's hand. 'Let's go and see Phelpy first.'

None of the children dared to call their father's assistant anything but Miss Phelps to her face. It was not so much that she was forbidding as unbending. For as long as they could remember anything about the *Wise Owl*, Miss Phelps had looked exactly the same. She had come on the day they had opened and except for an annual fortnight's holiday which she took at the end of September she had arrived punctually ever since at a quarter to nine every morning except Sundays. She had never told any of them anything about herself. Paul had once followed her to see where she lived and saw her go into an ugly villa in a dead-end street at the far end of the town. She always wore a blue serge dress in business and when working in her little glass box actually made and pinned on a pair of paper cuffs.

Her hair was sandy and her complexion pale and a trifle freckled. Her voice was unusually deep and had a surprising effect upon people who had not heard it before.

When they opened the house door into the shop Phelpy was dusting the books on the shelves with a feather duster.

'Good morning, Miss Phelps,' Veronica said politely. 'Our mother has had a mysterious letter and we're all sort of worried about it.'

'You don't sound it, child,' Phelpy boomed as she turned round. 'Good morning to you both,' and she continued to flip with the duster, working down the shelves past Literature, History and Biography to the big pile of green paper-covered mystery stories near the door.

'I don't think Daddy will be long,' Sally explained, 'but you will fetch him if you want him, won't you? . . . Are there any parcels yet? He said we could help unpack them if there are . . . Did you know I broke up yesterday, Miss Phelps? Are you looking forward to your holiday?'

'However much satisfaction one finds in one's work one always finds a change acceptable, Sally . . . No. The parcels have not yet arrived.'

Sally sighed and Veronica echoed her. Phelpy seemed even stiffer than usual this morning, so there didn't seem much sense in staying.

'If Paul comes down, will you please tell him that we've gone up to the vicarage?' and when Phelpy nodded the sisters went out together into the sunshine.

Nettleford was a pleasant little town with many gracious

buildings as old as the *Wise Owl*. Fifteen years ago a con-
crete by-pass road had been slashed across the county and
lucky Nettleford woke up one day to find itself compara-
tively isolated. There was nothing much to the town – a
pleasant river, a beautiful church, a commonplace cinema,
two handsome inns, a wide, tree-bordered High Street and
a gas-works and a railway station tucked away in the background. But although it was only eight miles from the
county town where Sally and Paul went to school, it
boasted a weekly market.

When Wilfred had first opened the *Wise Owl* most of his
neighbours had looked upon him as a harmless lunatic, but
it did not take long for the Richardsons to win everyone's
respect and the friendship of many, so that there were
plenty of smiles of welcome as Sally and Veronica strolled
down the street.

The chemist – or pharmacist as he called himself – who
had two enormous jars of glowing green and red at the
back of his window, greeted them from his step.

'What about the puppies, Mr Quirk?' Sally said. 'Have
they come yet? You did say I could have one, didn't you?'

'I did, Sally, and you shall. You shall have first pick.
Does your mother know she's going to have an addition to
the family?'

'Not yet, Mr Quirk. I was going to mention it to Daddy
first, but I don't think she'll mind – not much, anyway,
though I suppose it's a bit awkward upstairs. We've had
plenty of cats but never a dog, but I'm sure it will be all
right . . . Goodbye for the present.'

Next they met the vicar. Everybody liked him. Although
Mr Langton was extremely energetic he was round and

plump with bright eyes which twinkled at you through a most unusual pair of steel-rimmed glasses. Veronica once said—fortunately not in his hearing – that he reminded her of an 'extra fat robin in a hurry'.

'Hullo, you two,' he twittered. 'Broken up, I suppose? Yes, of course you have. What a stupid question . . . Elizabeth will be home this afternoon, so you'd better come in tomorrow, Sally. How's your father and mother? Good. Give them my love. I'm coming to see them soon, but I forget what about . . . Goodbye! Goodbye, my poppet' (this to Veronica). 'Here comes your brother. I must say he's looking extremely healthy . . . Goodbye to you all and Good morning to you, Mrs Starkens . . .' And with a beaming smile he hopped off the pavement almost as if he was hopping to another twig.

Paul saw them now and raised a hand in salutation.

'Where are you going and what for?' he demanded as he came up with his hands in his pockets.

'We don't know but we like it,' Veronica said. 'You go and catch your worms.'

'Sweet little thing. You've been teaching her manners, I can see, Sall, and just for your information I am going for worms, and Jimmy and me are then going to fish until lunch-time. After that we're *all* going to the farm to tea. Dad rang up just now when he came down to the shop. I like Northend and I like Uncle John Wilkins, but I warn you that Dad is in one of his moods and we shall all probably have to walk because he thinks we need the exercise and fresh air . . . Vee, of course, will go by bus with Mummy . . . Lucky little Vee . . . See you later, girls,' and he strolled off to find Jimmy.

2

NORTHEND EXPEDITION

NORTHEND FARM was five miles from Nettleford and lay snugly in a shallow valley about a mile from the main road. It had everything which a farm should have – a stream and a pond for ducks and geese; a rickyard with an easy entrance from the lane; two big barns with sagging roofs of warm, red tiles and some modern cowsheds, which were not so picturesque, out of sight behind them. Between the lane and the farmyard was a low wall – a lovely wall for sitting on or leaning against, with exciting cushions of moss and tiny flowers growing in the crumbling mortar between the bricks.

Northend had a good master. John Wilkins's great-grandfather had farmed the same land, and it was John's greatest grief that he had no child who would care for his precious acres when he had gone.

The Wilkins's friendship with the Richardsons had started about six months after the opening of the *Wise Owl*, when Wilfred had stopped one autumn evening to ask John the way back to Nettleford. He had explained that he was new to the district and was trying to explore it on foot when he could, but that today he had left his map at home. He had then added exactly the right thing by saying, 'I know nothing about your craft, sir, for I am a townsman, but if I owned and farmed land like this I should be not only very proud but very content.'

And John Wilkins, short and thick-set, with a battered

felt hat on the back of his head, had opened the gate and said, 'Maybe you'd like to look round. You've a mile up the lane to the main road where you can get a bus home so you'd better have a cup of tea before you do any more walking.'

Wilfred had looked round with genuine interest and pleasure, and had then followed his host into the stone-flagged kitchen, where he had been greeted like an old friend by Mary Wilkins, the farmer's wife. He had sat on a polished bench by the side of the range and eaten home-made bread and honey and drunk cup after cup of scalding tea. Mrs Wilkins had chattered and asked so many friendly questions that he had found himself telling them about Margaret and his family, and even of the adventure of the *Wise Owl*. Time slipped by. The curtains were drawn and the men lit their pipes and at last, when Wilfred with a sudden pang of conscience rose to go, John had said, 'Reckon it's good for us all to know something about the other chap's job. I'll be going round the farm in a few minutes, but I'll run you up to the bus stop in the car first ... Your missus'll be wondering what's happened to you ... Next time I'm in the town I'll come and look at your shop, and then maybe one day you can bring the young-sters out to see Mary here. She'd like that, wouldn't you, m'dear?'

That was how it started. A few days later John Wilkins, very smart in his market-day clothes, strolled into the *Wise Owl* and announced to a startled Miss Phelps, 'I want the governor, please, miss.'

Two Wednesdays later the Richardson children had been left with other friends and Wilfred had taken his wife to Northend. Margaret had been brought up in a country rectory and knew very much more about farms and farming people than her husband, so that the two women liked each other at once.

But farmers are busy people all through the year, and on Saturdays, Sundays and bank holidays too, and do not have time for much visiting. The Richardsons had no car, and it was only recently, when Veronica was old enough to walk a few miles, that they had all gone to Northend together. These excursions were great occasions, for to the children there were all the ever-new delights and surprises of the farm and the freedom of the country. The realization that they were allowed to explore the fields and woods as they liked so long as they closed all gates and broke no hedges was in itself a new adventure.

Then there were the farm animals. After a few visits and some encouragement from 'Uncle John' as she called him, Sally actually smacked a cow on its behind when it got in her way in the farmyard and was not instantly gored to death. Paul was fascinated by the tractors and the farm machines, and although Veronica did not care much for cows or tractors she had been known to stay by the pond for half an hour watching the ducks stand on their heads.

They all liked the men who worked there – old Tom, the stockman, whose job it was to look after the animals; cheeky young Bill, who drove the tractor and winked at Sally whenever he saw her; and Harry, the foreman, who, surprisingly, had a long, bushy moustache. There were others, too, for Northend was a big farm, but these three were the favourites.

And so, on this first Wednesday of the summer holidays,

as soon as Miss Phelps had put the dust sheets over the books and Wilfred had locked the door of the *Wise Owl* behind her, the Richardsons scrambled through a cold lunch as quickly as possible.

'Why you don't all suffer from indigestion I *don't* know,' Margaret said as Paul passed his plate for a third helping of potatoes. 'You eat like wolves. I shall have to consider giving you porridge for lunch. That might sober some of you . . . Did you catch many fish, Paul?'

'Not quite, Mum . . . Did you really mean that about porridge? I wouldn't mind trying it . . . Who's going to take Vee on the bus, or shall we all go that way and get there sooner? . . . May we all go by bus, Dad? It's jolly hot walking.'

'I'd like to walk all the way,' Veronica announced with feminine perversity. 'I'll wear my sandals.'

'Oh, shucks!' Paul said as he put down his knife and fork. 'You're crazy. You know you're tired after two miles . . . May we all go by bus, Dad?'

'I wonder why you use the expression "shucks", Paul?' his father said almost automatically. 'Where do you hear it and what does it mean? I do not wish to appear pedantic, but I would like you all —'

'To speak good English if you can,' Sally and Paul quoted together, and then the former got up and hugged her father.

'You're the most wonderful father, Daddy, but please don't be a fuss-pot on the first day of the holidays. Paul doesn't know where he hears things. He has the most awful friends. May we not wash up and all go by bus, please?'

Wilfred disentangled himself.

'Although I admonished you just now, Paul, I am sure that there are too many women in this house . . . Sally and Paul will wash up while your mother gets ready. We will all go by bus . . . We have fifteen minutes.'

Twelve minutes later Wilfred, in a light alpaca jacket, shabby flannel trousers, and his ancient panama hat, led his family to the bus stop. There was room on the top, and after Veronica had dragged Paul to the front seat, Sally sat down next to her mother.

'I want to ask you something, Mummy. That letter you had from Aunt Janet this morning. You looked worried. Has anything awful happened?'

Margaret laughed. 'Not yet, Sally. I'll tell you about it some time,' and Sally had to be content with that, but when they got off the bus at the top of the lane she lagged behind with Paul.

'Mummy won't tell me anything else about that letter from Aunt Janet. I've still got a feeling that there was something in it about us – or to do with us.'

'You're always wondering whether something terrible is going to happen, Sally.'

'The most awful thing about Aunt Janet is that one of us might be asked to go and stay there again. It's your turn next, anyway!' and she stopped in the middle of the road with a gasp of horror. 'Paul. You don't think it's anything to do with Tony!'

'Tony! That stuck-up sissy! Why should it be?'

'Just suppose that Aunt Janet has asked Mummy if he could come and stay with us these hols. She might do. She doesn't seem to understand how much we loathe him.

D'you remember when I had to go and stay with them that weekend before Christmas —'

Paul chuckled.

'Yes, I do. Didn't she write and say that as Tony hadn't any sisters you two would have lots of fun together? Did you?'

'You know I didn't, Paul. I told you when I came home how I hated every minute. Once, when I told Tony what I thought of him and his beastly swank he said something horrid about Dad and the *Wise Owl*. He sort of sneered because it was a shop . . . I slapped his face and he told Aunt Janet.'

'Yes, I remember now, Sall . . . Don't let's worry about him! Even if Aunt Janet suggests it we'll say we couldn't stick it, and I don't suppose he'll like the idea anyway.'

'I don't suppose he will. He's bigger than you, Paul. He's twelve.'

'Oh, shucks. It's a crazy idea. What made you think of it?'

'I don't know, but I wish I could forget it . . . Lend me your knife. I want to cut my initials on one of these beech trees.'

'You can't now. The others are waiting for us. Come on.'

The great beeches on the left of the lane were a glory all the year round. Wilfred said that he liked them best in winter when their graceful branches were bare against the clouds and their silver-grey trunks stretched upwards like the great stone columns in a cathedral. Margaret remembered them in May when the young leaves of pale green through which the light seemed to shine glistened against the clear, blue sky. Even Paul, who liked everything in the open air, but was not particularly interested in the names of trees or flowers or birds, was fascinated by the smooth texture of their bark and had carved his initials on three of them. Sally loved them best in autumn and winter when the leaves changed colour and seemed to give back all the sunshine they stored up during the summer. Only last October she had brought Veronica here and seen the trees blazing like a sunset sky. The leaves of gold and red and orange had crackled under their feet and they had filled their pockets with the little dark-brown triangular beech-nuts, some of which they had chewed on the way home. Later that evening round the fire Margaret had helped Veronica to thread the nuts on a short thread and wear them as a necklace.

At the top of the hill where the wood stopped as suddenly as it began, Margaret and Wilfred, with Veronica between them, were waiting by a gate. They nearly always stopped at this gate, for from its vantage point you could see right down into the valley with Northend Farm, like a toy model, lying in the hollow below. The lane, now with a tinkling stream at one side, wound its way down between hedgerows which were starred with the white blossom of brambles which soon would turn to a harvest of black-berries. Far away on the opposite slope of the valley was a wood and a few cottages, but the fields themselves, soft-ened in the heat haze, now glowed with the rich gold of ripening grain.

'I wonder when Uncle John begins to cut all this,' Paul said. 'I'm going to ask him if we can come over this year. I like to see the rabbits bolting when they get to the middle of the field. Will you make a rabbit-pie if I catch some, Mum? I shall ask Bill if I can ride on the tractor, too.'

'Bill promised me,' Sally said. 'Weeks and weeks ago, the last time we came over, he promised that I should.'

'I dare say there'll be room for you both,' Margaret smiled. 'What are you going to do, Vee?'

'Ducks,' said her younger daughter tersely. 'Let's go.'

Half-way down the hill they caught up Tom, the stockman, ambling along behind some black and white cows. He moved a stumpy pipe from his mouth, touched his old hat, and grunted a greeting, and they followed him down to the farmyard.

The farmhouse at Northend stood back from the lane about fifty yards and was approached by a gravel path which was wide enough for the old car. On the right of the 'drive', as Mary Wilkins called it, was a lawn and some flower beds and this little fragment of Northend's acres was her own special domain. She cut the grass herself with a hand-mower, scorning her husband's rather half-hearted offers of help, and trimmed the edges and pruned her beloved roses in season. She had a little greenhouse, too, and in this she raised her seedlings with loving care.

Almost as soon as Christmas had gone the first snowdrops and golden winter aconites greeted another year in Mary Wilkins's garden. Then came the other bulbs and on Easter Day there were no finer daffodils to decorate the church than those from Northend. But roses were, perhaps, her special joy, and when the Richardsons opened the gate this afternoon she was working among them. She looked up at the sound of the latch and her face beamed with pleasure as Veronica raced across the grass.

33

'We're early, Aunt Mary. We came by bus 'cos we were in such a hurry to get here.'

'Bless my soul,' said Mary Wilkins as she put down her basket and scissors. 'You're much too early for us, miss. Much too early. We can't put up with you at this time. Back you go where you came from.'

Then she greeted the others, and when Wilfred had admired the flowers he wandered off to find the farmer.

'I'm going to see the cows. They'll be milking now,' Sally said. 'What about you, Vee?'

'I'm going to do ducks, thank you. I can do them quite easily by myself. All I want is a bag of bread . . . I wonder where Paul is going?'

Paul was already at the gate.

'I'm going to find Bill and fix him about the tractor,' he shouted, and ran down the lane before Sally realized that he had deserted her.

He glanced up the hill to the left and saw his father walking with long strides up the side of the hedge towards the wood. Then he stood still for a moment wondering whether the throb of a tractor would lead him to Bill. It was very quiet and for a few minutes all that he could hear was that strange hum of a myriad insects and bees that countrymen call 'midsummer hum'.

Then, quite suddenly, the silence was broken by a bellowing and shouting away behind the barns, and a flock of rooks, disturbed by the noise, rose cawing in protest out of the elm tree under which he was standing.

Paul ran back along the lane and into the big, square farmyard which was bounded by the two barns, a stable and a huge, open shed where the farm machines were kept.

As he slammed the gate behind him, his friend Bill got up from beside a tractor which he had been repairing and ran out through the other gate leading to the rickyard. As the hubbub increased Paul shouted, 'Wait for me, Bill,' but the man did not even hear him.

He followed as quickly as he could, but stopped when he saw what was happening in the paddock behind the barns. Several men, including Tom, the stockman, were struggling with a huge bull and trying to force it back into its shed. Paul knew this bull well enough and had often hoisted himself up so that he could look over the half-door and watch the enormous animal chewing placidly in his stall. He had always seemed quiet and peaceful enough, but now he was very angry, for he was tossing his great head and pawing the ground as the men closed round him. Then Paul noticed that Tom had in his hand a pole with a hook on one end and was just edging a little nearer when the farmer himself came running up the paddock.

'Get out of here, Paul,' he shouted when he saw the boy.

Paul knew Uncle John well enough to realize that he meant what he said, so he edged back towards the gate. But he did go very slowly and saw Tom thrust the end of his pole through the ring on the unfortunate bull's nose, and in less than a minute the bellowing victim was safe back again in his shed. As soon as the door was securely latched Paul sidled forward again.

'Nar then, young 'Arry,' he heard Tom say, and watched in fascination as the burly stockman thrust his huge moustache almost in the face of a pale, rather shifty-looking farm-hand whom Paul had not seen before. 'Nar then! 'Ow many times 'ave Oi told you to shut that

35

blamed door . . . A 'nundred times, I reckon . . . Tole you till Oi be near black in the face . . . Yer that careless yer not to be trusted anywhere . . .'

Paul could not hear the other's reply, but he saw Uncle John step between the two men and wave the others away.

'Shucks, Bill! What happened?' he said as the tractor man came up to him.

Bill laughed.

'So you've turned up again, have you, my lad? . . . Nothing much happened except young Harry let the bull out. I hopes as how you couldn't hear all that Tom was saying to him. I've never heard anybody called so many different things as old Tom called Harry when he heard the bull was out . . . The guvnor's giving Harry a bit o' news about himself now, I shouldn't wonder . . . Care to come and hold a spanner for me? There's plenty o' work for me just now getting everything ready for harvest.'

On their way back to the big shed they met Sally on her way to the cows, and Veronica, with a large paper bag clasped to her middle, heading for the duck pond.

'Hullo, Bill,' the former said with a shameless smile. 'It's lovely to see you again . . . You did promise to let me ride on the tractor with you at harvest-time, didn't you?'

'Maybe you'll have to ask the guvnor first, but it's all right with me. I'll take you for a ride any time, Sally . . . Are you going to stay and talk to the engineers? We'd like your company.'

'Not for me, thanks,' Paul said. 'I have it every day. Sally's no good on a tractor, Bill. The shaking up and down makes her sick, and I know she doesn't like the smell of oil like I do. You take me as your mate, Bill.'

But Bill wisely would not commit himself, so Sally wandered off to the milking shed, with a mocking smile for her brother.

Later they all met for tea which Aunt Mary and Margaret brought out to the lawn under the shade of a chestnut tree.

Paul had squashed his third wasp before he asked the question which had been on his lips all the afternoon.

'When you start your harvest, Uncle John, we'd like to come and help you – Sally and me, I mean. Could we?'

' 'Tis hard work, but you'd both be welcome if you'd stick it. I may be glad of help as I sacked young Harry just now, Mary. He's asked for his cards and I've settled with him.'

'I'm sorry,' Mary said. 'I hope you didn't lose your temper, John.'

' 'Fraid I did, Mary. I can't get rid of that devil of mine, can I? Nothing makes me more angry than slackness and carelessness on the farm. That fellow's no good anyway. His mind isn't on his work. Tom says he's been slacking for weeks, and today he let the bull out – left the door open, if you please, after taking in his feed . . . He answered me back so I told him he could go.'

'I hope you haven't been too hasty. One of the women told me Harry was in some sort of trouble at home . . . And if these youngsters do come over later just try and remember that they're not as strong as you . . . Now, Veronica, my love, 'tis time you started on my Angel cake.'

After tea the men and Paul went off with two guns to shoot rabbits at the edge of the wood. Wilfred was, in truth, secretly afraid of his weapon and not at all fond of slaughtering rabbits, but he wanted to be a countryman if he could, so he did his best, which was not very good. Veronica went into the kitchen with her mother and Aunt Mary, while Sally, feeling once again that she wanted to be a dairymaid, went off to the cowsheds to watch the men washing down, and it did not seem long before they finished and the hunters came back with four rabbits.

'I have perhaps fired twenty of our friend's cartridges, which seems to be rather wasteful,' Wilfred remarked ruefully, 'but I have slaughtered this little beast. It will make only a very small pie, Margaret.'

'I should stuff it, darling, and keep it in the study. Or perhaps you would rather suspend it over the mantelpiece? Isn't that what the best sportsmen do?'

When at last it was time to go, John offered to take them home in the car, but they preferred to walk to the main road.

'I'll be ringing you up when I'm ready for help,' Uncle John said to Paul and Sally. 'Some time towards the end of the week, I reckon. Just a few more days of this sun and this year's harvest won't be so bad.'

'That means 'twill be about best ever,' his wife laughed. 'Goodbye all, and we'll see you soon I hope.'

As they walked up the hill, slowly because of Veronica, the bats fluttered crazily round their heads as the sun went down, and when they turned by the gate for a final glimpse of the farm the last rays touched the red roofs with a finger of fire so that they glowed in sudden splendour.

3

THE NETTLEFORD OWLERS

The next day began quite normally.

Sally and Paul both slept on late and there were no good deeds such as tea-making before breakfast. Both had been called before their father went into the bathroom and there was the usual scuffle to get in first after he had gone. Sally won without much difficulty, and remembered to take her tooth-paste with her when she went upstairs to finish dressing.

Veronica scrambled into her chair as her mother brought in the eggs and Wilfred settled down to his paper without even looking at his pile of letters.

They had all reached the marmalade stage when the blow fell.

'What are you going to do this morning, Sally?' Margaret asked.

'Going round to the vicarage as soon as poss., Mum. Elizabeth's home and we promised to meet this morning.'

'Of course. But I do want you to help me for a while after breakfast. We shall have to get the camp bed into your room for Veronica as we must have her room for Tony tomorrow.'

Wilfred put down his paper and looked at them all over his spectacles, giving the impression that he was waiting for the storm to burst. Only Veronica seemed unmoved for she merely murmured, 'I like sleeping with Sall. She can read to me in the mornings.'

Paul dropped his knife with a clatter. 'Shucks, Mum! You don't mean *Tony – tomorrow*? Why – it's so soon. It's almost here now. *Must* he come?'

Sally's face was white.

'But Mummy, you don't really mean it? You know we don't like him. It's a terrible thing you're saying. It isn't as if it was somebody we liked . . . And are you really sure that he wants to come to us? I can't believe he does.'

Margaret put down her cup.

'I can't quite believe it, either, but Aunt Janet and your uncle are going abroad for three weeks – it's been arranged suddenly – and they have asked me if we will have Tony. They cannot leave him alone in the flat and it seems that there isn't anywhere else for him to go. I don't think he has many friends – you must remember that it isn't as easy for an only child to make friends as it is for you . . . Your father and I have talked this over and we think that we should have him here and we know that you will back us up and make him welcome.'

'Who *is* Tony?' Veronica asked. 'I can't remember him.'

'We don't *want* anyone else here, Mum,' Paul said. 'We all get on all right. I've got Jimmy and the fishing and Sall has got Elizabeth, and then sometimes we do things together and soon we're going to Wales —' He stopped as Sally pushed back her chair and stood up.

'Don't hide anything else,' she said bitterly. 'Is he coming with us to Tenby? It's bad enough to have to put up with him here, but if he's coming with us on our precious holiday then I don't know what I'll do,' and to her fury she felt the tears in her eyes.

'Sit down, darling,' her mother said, 'and don't be dramatic. I think we can squeeze him in at Tenby so he must come with us. We would much rather go on our own, of course, but this is something we think we ought to do ... And you mustn't talk in this ridiculous way as if you hated each other.'

'You don't understand,' Sally muttered through a mouthful of toast. 'You're grown up and you don't understand how we feel about him. He's a prig and stuck-up because they've got more money than we have, and he doesn't like the sort of things we do here. How could he? ... And what are we going to do with him? Do you think he'll get any fun out of coming shopping with you and stopping to talk to Mr Quirk on his doorstep and Mrs Venables at the vegetable stall? Do you think Paul wants him to go fishing and —'

'Sally!' her father spoke quite sharply. 'You forget yourself. Finish your breakfast, please.'

But later when she was helping to put up the camp bed in her room her mother spoke to her again.

'I'm sorry about this, Sally. You said downstairs when you were in a temper that it's difficult for me to understand how you feel about Tony because I'm grown up ... It's just because you're not yet grown up that perhaps you don't understand how I feel about helping my sister, Janet, by having Tony here. I know that up to now he hasn't fitted in with us and I know that you didn't enjoy yourself when you went up to them in London at Christmas, but he is your cousin —'

'I don't see that's got anything to do with it,' Sally interrupted as she pulled the sheet taut on her side of the bed.

'Just because you have relations it doesn't mean that you have to like them. Besides, we know people like Uncle John Wilkins and Aunt Mary, who aren't relations at all but are marvellous . . . So why do we have to bother about a boy like Tony when he doesn't like us?'

Margaret sighed.

'Just because your father and I think it is our duty to have him here. When you are older I'm sure you'd do anything you could to help Paul because he's your brother. That's how I feel about my sister.'

Sally felt this argument to be unfair. Grown-ups often argued in this way and it was particularly difficult to tell her mother that she wouldn't feel like doing anything much for Paul if she disliked him half as much as she detested Tony!

'Oh well!' she said. 'I think it's one of the most terrible things you've ever done to us and you'll soon see that he won't really want to be with us either. I can't bear to think of Tenby now. When is he coming, Mummy? Not until this evening I hope?'

Margaret came round to Sally's side of the bed, put her arm round her shoulders and pulled her down beside her.

'Stop being a martyr, Sally. Cheer up and make the best of it. Tony is coming whether you and Paul like it or not, and whether I like it or not. Can't you see that I would rather have you all on my own in the holidays than include a visitor? We're not doing this for fun, but because we think we should . . . I don't expect Tony is too bad really and almost everybody is nicer when they see that you're trying to like them . . . Just try and grow up, Sally darling, and make the best of this. We shall expect you and Paul not to let us down ... Tony is due at five. You and Paul must meet him but you can run off now if you like. Don't be late for lunch and give my love to Elizabeth ... Where's Paul? Fishing?'

She dropped a kiss on the top of Sally's head and added, 'Don't take yourself so seriously, Sall!'

Sally smiled ruefully.

'All right. You're a wonderful wheedler, Mummy. I'll try. Paul is with Jimmy and I expect they've both fallen in the river by now. He's never very far from water except the sort you wash and bathe in ... I'll try not to be late for lunch but Liza and I have got a lot to talk about.'

She went out through the shop but her father was busy with a customer so she could not speak to him, and the thought of Tony receded as she strolled down the sunny High Street towards the vicarage.

'Good morning, Mr Quirk. What about the puppies? Any news yet?'

'Not yet, my dear. About ten days now. How's your Dad?'

Outside the ironmonger's she stopped for a word with Jimmy's father who was busy arranging some of his wares on the pavement.

'Have you seen my brother please, Mr Brand? I suppose he's gone off with Jimmy?'

Mr Brand, who was as sandy and freckled as his son, nodded gloomily. 'Two of 'em each as crazy as the other, Sally. They've gone off with two rods bigger than themselves and enough line to hang themselves with ... How's your mother?'

She nodded a welcome to the cobbler who worked close

to the window of his little shop and kept a supply of nails in his mouth, and waved to the stout Mrs Venables with her vegetable stall on the other side of the street, and then turned in at the vicarage drive. The old house needed a coat of paint, but it looked very gracious in the sunshine with a shadow from the great cedar tree on the lawn stretching out towards the pillared porch. The front door was open and Sally walked straight in.

A thin little woman, with straggling, grey hair, was speaking on the telephone in the hall and almost beating time with a long cigarette holder as she did so. She smiled at Sally when she recognized her but went on with the conversation.

'. . . I daresay the vicar will sign the form for you, although I don't think he knows you . . . Yes! Yes! You've told me your name, Mrs Green, and where you live, but I still don't think he knows you . . . You don't come to church do you? – Pardon? "Not exactly" . . . How very odd. Do you or don't you? . . . You don't? And if the vicar signs your form you might consider it? How nice of you, but I don't think that idea would appeal at all to my husband . . . You think we're unreasonable? . . . Oh! You've gone . . . Hullo, Sally, my dear. How are you? That was such a rude woman on the telephone. She wanted the vicar to call and sign a form for her . . . Elizabeth is in her room trying to get tidy. Run up and find her.'

Elizabeth Langton was a few months younger than Sally and as fair as her friend was dark. She had an impudent little face and looked as if she might one day be as plump as her father. She had two brothers – Hugh, who

44

was five, and Charles just fifteen, who went to a public school.

The two girls had been friends for four years – ever since the Langtons had come to Nettleford.

Sally liked writing letters and although Elizabeth hated putting pen to paper she nearly always wrote back. But this term she had not been so good at replying and Sally was feeling a little peevish with her as she climbed the stairs and ran down the broad corridor towards her room.

Elizabeth was sitting on her bed with sunshine playing round her fair head. Every drawer and every cupboard door was open and the floor was covered with her unpacking which spilled from her open trunk like a cascade.

'Hullo, Sall,' she grinned without getting up. 'I hoped it was you. I'm fed up with this. Let's go out.'

Sally stood in the doorway trying to look stern. 'Why didn't you answer my letters, Liza? You owe me two.'

'Don't be silly, Sall. Don't start the hols. like that. Are you trying to be dramatic?'

Sally flushed. This was the second time she had been told that in half an hour.

'Why didn't you, anyway? It's just because it's a trouble I s'pose. You don't mind me sitting down at night after I've done my prep. and telling you all about the things that happen here, but you can't even bother to reply . . .'

Elizabeth got up from the bed, stretched her arms over her head and began to throw her clothes back into the trunk.

'You *are* an idiot, Sall. Do stop fussing. You know I hate writing letters. I'd ring you up except that I never have any money and I don't think your father would like it if I reversed the charge . . . Come out under the cedar and talk. I've got a wonderful idea . . .'

It was impossible to be cross with Elizabeth for long and by the time they reached the shade of the great tree on the lawn she had told Sally that Charles did not arrive until tomorrow and was then bringing a friend with him, and had also heard the news about Tony.

'I came round to see you last night, Sall. 'Bout eight, I s'pose, but the *Wise Owl* was shut up and nobody answered the bell. Even if I'm not good at letters you see that I remember my friends. I thought you'd have been round here or waited in for me. I telephoned first but although there wasn't an answer I came just the same.'

Sally flung herself on the tarnished grass and looked up at the gnarled branches above her.

'I don't believe you, Liza. You're making it all up. If you *did* telephone and there wasn't any reply you're much too lazy to come round . . . Now tell me your idea. I want to hear something wonderful to help me forget Tony.'

Elizabeth rolled over, picked a daisy and held it between her teeth, but before she could answer her mother came out of the front door and called, 'Have you tidied your room, darling, and put all your things away?'

Liza got to her knees and waved.

'Sally has come, Mummy. Isn't it lovely?' and Mrs Langton waved vaguely and went indoors again.

'That's all right, Sall. Don't look so priggish. I didn't say I had tidied up and you can come and help me presently . . . Now listen and I'll tell you my idea . . . What we want here in the holidays is a Secret Club . . . Oh, I know that years and years ago when we were kids we

had something – we called ourselves the Peewits, didn't we? – but this ought to be different. We'll have a code for writing to each other —"

'I thought you hated writing letters,' Sally interrupted. 'You can't write ordinary words properly so I can't think how you'll ever manage a code. I think this is a silly idea.'

'So you think the whole idea is silly, do you? I needn't have troubled to tell you. What's happened to you this term, Sall?'

'I don't think the idea of a Secret Club is silly, but your idea of a code. You'd lose the answer to the code and we'd all be doing work for nothing. I know you. You're hopeless, Liza . . . Go on. Tell me the rest. What shall we do with the Club and who's going to be in it?'

'I'm not sure yet what we shall do but we'll have a proper meeting-place, secret from the grown-ups, and we'll have rules and a secret sign so that we'll recognize each other. All right. Don't say it. I can see you looking superior – and I had an idea that we might use the Club really for helping other people.'

Sally looked at her suspiciously.

'Sort of Robin Hood?'

'Not exactly. And not for helping people all the time. We should do other things of course.'

'What things?'

'Don't be such a misery, Sall. It's not like you, and I don't like you much.'

'I'm sorry, Liza. It's the idea of this Tony coming I s'pose. He'll spoil everything. We'll never be able to go anywhere without him. He'll be like the albatross in *The Ancient Mariner*.'

'I read that once,' Liza said. 'I liked the way the words went. Something about "Water, water, everywhere, and not a drop to drink", and "a painted ship upon a painted ocean" . . . I remember the albatross, too. I see what you mean . . . Anyway it's silly to ask what we'll do. We can think of things to do as we go along and you can ask Tony to join and I expect he'll say "No", and then we'll know where we are.'

'No, we shan't. If he says "Yes", it will be awful and if he refuses we shall still have to be with him.'

'That's when we shall want the code then,' Elizabeth said triumphantly. 'We'll write messages to each other and he'll be mad because he can't translate them . . . Who shall we have in it? Only people we can trust and not too many to begin with.'

When they talked it over further it didn't seem as if it was going to be a very big club. There was no doubt that Veronica and Hugh were too young, and although secretly Sally thought Charles was wonderful, he was certainly too old.

'We'll ask Paul,' Liza said. 'He's fun. I like him.'

'I don't suppose he'll join unless Jimmy does. Jimmy Brand. Red-headed and freckled. He's in your father's choir and I'm sure you remember him. They're both crazy on fishing at the moment but I expect it will be caterpillars tomorrow. Would you mind Jimmy?'

'I don't think so. Let's go and find them and see what they think. We can start with four.'

They found the two boys half an hour later on the river bank under some willows. Jimmy Brand was squatting on his haunches and gazing fixedly at a scarlet float which was bobbing about in the eddies. Paul was stretched on his stomach with his nose only about nine inches above the water and his rod held firmly in both hands. Each boy had a bottle of fizzy lemonade, a packet of sandwiches and a small tin of worms by his side.

'Hullo!' Sally said brightly. 'We thought we'd like to see how you did it and besides that we've got an idea.'

Jimmy looked round, nodded and then went on hypnotizing his float. Paul was not even amused.

'Why did you have to come and find us? Can't you see how busy we are? Don't say Tony has arrived already . . . Hullo, Elizabeth. It's you is it?'

'Yes it is, and just remember we've walked miles in this boiling sun just to tell you our idea. You ought to be jolly pleased instead of being rude.'

'I'm not pleased. I'm sorry, but I'm just not. Fishing isn't a thing for girls.'

They won the boys round in the end and a quarter of an hour later they were all sharing the sandwiches which had been provided by Mrs Brand. Paul was surprisingly keen on the Club idea.

'I think it's a jolly good scheme,' he mumbled through a mouthful of bread. 'We can have different meeting-places and go to them quite secretly and make some rules and do things which nobody knows about.'

'Liza wants to help people,' Sally said. 'I s'pose she means rob the rich to help the poor, but everybody we know is poor.'

'We could do good stealthily,' Elizabeth suggested.

'You start with Tony then,' Paul grinned. 'You can have

him at the vicarage. It wouldn't be very stealthy but it would be doing good to us.'

'We could make a secret camp,' Jimmy said in his abrupt way, 'and light fires and cook grub and maybe sleep out. We could go exploring and follow trails and watch suspicious strangers. I reckon it's a smashing idea . . . I got a name for us, too. You two come from the *Wise Owl* so we'll be the Owlers . . . When shall we start?'

Elizabeth looked at him admiringly.

'I think that's pretty good, Jimmy. Let us have the first meeting this afternoon in our attic at the vicarage. There's plenty of room and none of the others come up there and we'll make rules and swear an awful oath of secrecy.'

'Sorry to keep asking awkward questions,' Sally said, 'but how? I mean, how do we get to your attic without being seen? It seems rather an odd place to go.'

'No, it isn't really. You three meet at the gate in the back garden at half-past two. If it's unlocked then you'll know it's all right and you can come up to the scullery door. Dad will be in his study and we shall have washed up the lunch things so Mother will be in her room. I shan't unlock the gate until the coast is clear. All we'll have to do is go up the back stairs to the attic where I'll have everything ready. Now you boys can get on with your fishing. Come on, Sall. We'll go and buy an ice.'

'Pigs,' Paul said as he lifted his rod tenderly. 'You've eaten all our sandwiches, too.'

Lunch at the *Wise Owl* was a peaceful meal – so peaceful that Margaret was suspicious because there was no mention at all of Tony.

'You've been hiding from me all the morning, Sall,'

Veronica said, 'but I don't care what you do this afternoon. I'm going out with Mummy.'

'That reminds me,' Margaret said. 'We'll have tea
after Tony arrives. I want Sally and Paul to meet him
at the station. Five o'clock train. You won't forget, will
you?'

'I'm sure we shan't,' Sally said meekly. 'We've got an
important appointment at half-past two, but I'm sure we
shall be free by five. I don't think our business will take
longer than that, will it, Paul?'

Paul didn't think so and smiled cheerfully when his
father looked surprised.

Jimmy was waiting for them outside the garden door of
the vicarage. He had changed out of his angling clothes
and his sandy hair looked darker than usual because he
had smoothed it down with water.

'Up the Owlers,' he whispered. 'The door's O.K. I've
tried it.'

They scuttled up the garden path between the over-
grown shrubs and reached the yard at the back of the
house. Sally's heart was thumping ridiculously but she
smiled to herself when she remembered that the only
people whom they were really trying to avoid were her
friends. Elizabeth was waiting for them just inside her
scullery.

'The coast is clear,' she whispered.

She led them into the kitchen and up two flights of
narrow, uncarpeted stairs to the top floor which had been
used in the days when there had been servants in the
vicarage. On one side of the passage were three small
unused bedrooms, and on the other an attic under a sloping

roof, divided into two. Elizabeth opened the door of the latter.

'There's a lot of junk in here so do be careful, and the electric light doesn't work,' she whispered. 'Our place is at the far end, through another door.'

'Have we got to do everything in the dark?' Paul whispered as he stumbled against an old trunk, 'and I I don't want to be rude but it's fairly warm up here.'

'Fairly warm' was not a very adequate description. It was sweltering.

'Don't be funny,' Elizabeth said. 'And do be careful. There's a little window in our room. Let me get at the door.'

'There's a very rum noise,' Jimmy whispered through clenched teeth. 'Is anyone else here?'

They stood still in the dark and listened.

'Idiot. It's the water tank. It always gurgles. Come on . . .'

Then Jimmy tripped over a pair of skating boots, clutched at Sally and they both fell down with a clatter.

'Shucks!' Paul gasped. 'You two would. I hope you've hurt yourselves.'

Elizabeth had now reached the inner door which she opened so that there was enough light for Sally and Jimmy to pick themselves up and scuttle into sanctuary. This attic was long and narrow, with such a steeply sloping roof that none of them could stand upright except by the wall. At the far end, opposite the door, was a small window, smothered in cobwebs, overlooking the back garden. The atmosphere was stifling and thick with dust.

'If we can ever get here without being noticed I should

think this is secret enough,' Sally gasped as she wiped her face with a grubby handkerchief. 'Does the window open?'

Paul was already struggling with it and when, at last, after several terrific bangs on the sash, it flew open they all crowded round and gulped in the fresh air gratefully. It was Jimmy who noticed that from this window they could look right down into the branches of a tree growing against the wall of the house.

'If we had a thread on a pulley and a tin fixed on the end of the thread,' he gasped when he had struggled back, 'we could send messages up and down.'

'You look very, very hot, Jimmy,' Sally said. 'Are you feeling all right except for that, because what you're saying sounds crazy?'

'I done this sort of thing before, Sall. It's potty. S'pose one day Liza was waiting up here for us and we couldn't come or we wanted to send her some sort of message. All we have to do is to write her a note – in code of course. We must have a code —'

'I've got one,' Paul interrupted. 'A super one.'

'So have I. I got six codes . . . Anyway, we come through the garden gate if the coast is clear to the tree right under this window, where we'll be hidden from the house and garden too. Nobody except us will know there's a tin or a match-box on the end of a thread between the tree and the wall, and we put the paper in and pull the string and up goes the message to the window-sill here, where Liza takes it in. If she wants she can send a reply down same way . . . It's easy. I'll fix it soon as you like.'

They looked at him admiringly. Only Elizabeth seemed doubtful.

'But how do I know when a message is coming up? I can't spend all day here – I mean I'll want to do something else sometimes.'

Jimmy was undaunted.

'You'll have to be here at a special time and then I'll fix a little bell I got for fishing rods on to the pulley up here. When we pulls the thread down below the bell tinkles up here. It's potty. Honestly it is . . . Golly it's hot! I'm going to take off my shirt.' And he did.

After that they tried to settle down to business. Sally had brought a notebook and pencil and although they all found it difficult to decide just exactly what the Owlers were really *for*, they were all certain that they must exist and that something would, sooner or later, turn up for them to do. But it was very hot in the attic and they would all rather have been out in the garden or by the river, and that was why the rules in Sally's notebook were rather sketchy. They read like this –

SECRET RULES OF THE NETTLEFORD OWLERS

(1) This is a secret Club and all members swear to keep it secret, specially from grown-ups.

(2) The first four members are Elizabeth Ann Langton, Sally Margaret Richardson, Paul David Richardson, James Alfred Brand.

(3) There can be other members if the other members all agree.

(4) All the members (specially the first four) swear to be true to each other whatever happens till death do us part.

(5) The Club is for organizing things for ourselves and for doing things secretly to help other people.

(6) There is to be a code for writing to each other.

(7) We can add any more rules we think are good.

'But don't let's do any more now,' Paul gasped as his sister wrote down the last. 'I can't stick it up here any longer. This is a grand Club and the rules are good, but let's go down by the river to a place we know and I'll show you the code.'

The house was still quiet as they groped their way out to the landing and down the back stairs into the garden again. Nettleford itself seemed asleep too. On the sunny side of the broad High Street the shop blinds were drawn over the pavement and on the other the shadows of the houses were cool and inviting. A haze of heat shimmered over the roadway.

They crossed the bridge at the end of the town and turned along the path by the side of the little river. The water, dappled invitingly by the shadows of the over-hanging trees, moved lazily at their feet, and their sandals made no sound as they walked in single file without speaking until Paul, who was leading, turned aside from the track when it made a short-cut for a bend in the stream, and parted the overhanging branches of a weeping-willow.

'We found this a long time ago,' he said. 'Your attic is a wonderful idea, Liza, but it's too hot for it today. You can sit under the trees on the bank and put your feet in the water if you like.'

'It's wonderful,' Sally agreed as she slipped off her sandals. 'It's like a green tent.'

They sat there together with the cool, clear water flowing gently over their dusty feet, and peering through the screen of quivering willow leaves to the meadows on the other side of the stream. Suddenly a kingfisher, in a dazzling flash of royal blue, skimmed over the water.

'If it wasn't so hot I'd find where that chap lives,' Jimmy murmured as he lay back luxuriously. 'They always hunt the same part of the river. We might have called ourselves kingfishers, I s'pose, but Owlers will do . . . We shall have to have a secret sign for all our documents. One day maybe we could make a seal. I'll try and Dad would help without knowing what it was . . . Tonight I'll make the pulley and we'll fix it tomorrow if you like, Liza.'

'Tomorrow,' Sally sighed. 'Tomorrow we shall have Tony. What *shall* we do about him, Paul?'

'I'd forgotten him and we've got to be at the station at five. I wonder what the time is?'

'I don't care,' Sally said. 'I just don't care. I want to stay here for ever.'

'Is he so awful really?' Elizabeth asked. 'I mean, can't you do anything with him? Wouldn't he want to do any of the things we do? I don't want him in the Owlers, but if you can't ever leave him behind it might be better to make him a holiday member. We needn't tell him the code. Why don't you wait and see what he's like and if he's not too bad you could ask him if he would like to join a secret club? If he's all right we'll make him a half-member.'

'Let's forget him for another hour,' Sally said. 'One of you boys show us a code.'

Paul got in first. Jimmy was nearly always a little slow to speak.

57

'Let me have that old exercise book, Sall, and your pencil. My code is easy to remember and jolly difficult to work out. Tell me a number under ten somebody? Seven? Right. That's our key number and the smart thing about this code is that it can be altered every day if we like ... Look! It's easy. S'pose Sally and me want to meet you two at four o'clock next Wednesday in this place, what sort of message would we write ...'

He turned over a page of the notebook and pressed so hard with the pencil that the point snapped. Then he wrote with the stump.

'Meet Sall and me urgent Wednesday four at willow tree by river tell James.'

'I like the last word,' Jimmy said. 'Nobody ever calls me that except Dad when he's mad with me.'

'I put that to make it more difficult ... Do get back a bit, Liza. Your hair's tickling my face.'

Elizabeth sat back on her heels obediently. She was too intrigued to protest at such rudeness.

'This is how we do it,' Paul went on struggling with the blunted point. 'Seven is our key number so we make the words of our message the seventh every time, in a jumble of other words ... Like this –

ELEPHANTS ALWAYS TOAST MANCHESTER AN ONCE MEET OFTEN WINDOWS ON OAKS AND BICYCLES SALL AND THE END AND ALWAYS WHALES AND I HATE TO TELL YOU LIVERPOOL ME —'

'That *is* good,' Sally said. 'It's *jolly* good, isn't it, Liza? What a smart little brother I've got.'

'That's nothing,' Jimmy protested. 'I know that one.

It's easy. I'll show you another when we get tired of that one.'

'Of course we can change,' Paul said generously, 'but you do see how this works don't you? If you underline the seventh word every time you can see the message . . . "*Meet – Sall – and – me*" – and of course we could change the key number every day.'

'That would be awful,' Liza said. 'I should never re-member which day fitted which number, but let's agree the first number now. Say, three, and finish the first message we send to each other with the next number to be the next day.'

They agreed to three and on Liza's idea and stayed for a little longer watching the kingfisher.

'I s'pose we ought to go soon,' Sally sighed. 'I s'pose you and Jimmy wouldn't like to come to the station with us? Don't you think the Owlers ought to stick together, Liza?'

'Not as much as that, Sall. We'll have to meet your Tony of course, but I don't think it would be fair to the boy to meet us all together. What do you think, Jimmy?'

Jimmy, as Paul had done earlier, was now lying on his stomach, with his face a few inches above the water.

'Wish I'd brought the tackle along,' he murmured. 'I can almost catch 'em in my fingers . . . Pity you can't stay, Paul. I think I'll go for my rod.'

They went back together and parted at the bridge.

'You must let me know how you get on with him,' Eliza-beth said. 'Shall I ring you up tonight? I'm jolly curious about your Tony. Maybe I'll walk along towards the station presently and meet you all by mistake.'

'You can if you like,' Paul grinned. 'Dad gave me the money for a taxi 'cos dear Tony is sure to come with a lot of luggage.'

'All right. We'll meet tomorrow. If you don't come round in the morning I'll see Jimmy and then we'll leave a code message in the *Wise Owl*. Is the key number seven or three, Paul?'

'Three till we change it . . . Come on, Sall. Let's get it over. It's a quarter to five . . . Leave some fish in the river, Jim, and think of us being polite to our visitor.'

The station, nearly a mile from the town, was quite a peaceful place. Paul liked it for a number of reasons. He liked to see the expresses rocking through with the driver, in a cap with a shiny, black peak, peering from the cab. He liked to see the gleaming rails stretching straight up the gradient until they narrowed to one bright point. He liked the way the platforms stood high above the road so that he could look right over the water meadows to the church tower. He liked Ernest, the old porter, and Mr Robinson, who looked after the book-stall and wore a greenish bowler hat on the back of his head throughout summer and winter.

This afternoon the heat of the sun was enough to sizzle the creosote on the railway sleepers and the smell was familiar and very pleasant.

Sally, who had been admiring the hollyhocks, standing so straight to attention against the black fence, strolled over to the seat and sat down. She jumped up with a yell of surprise.

'Don't sit on that, Paul. It's red-hot. I've burnt the back of my legs.'

Her brother was looking up the line.

'What's he like, Sall? To look at, I mean. I've forgotten.'

'I saw him at Christmas. Maybe he'll look different in the summer. He always had jolly expensive clothes and he has lots of pocket-money.'

'His face, I mean. How will we know him?'

'Oh! His face. I don't think there's much to remember really. His teeth stick out a bit and so does his nose and his hair is sort of mousey. I don't really know what he looks like except that he had pimples at Christmas and his face is pale . . . He's much *bigger* than you, Paul . . . Here's Ernest coming over . . . Train must be due.'

A bell tinged in the signal-box and two signals fell. Far away, up the hill, as far as they could see, a tiny plume of smoke heralded their doom.

'I feel like saying "Goodbye" to everything,' Sally said breathlessly. 'We'll stick together over this, won't we? I mean just because he's a boy you won't go off with him . . . Sorry, Paul. That was idiotic of me.'

Had they known it, their cousin Tony, now dragging two heavy suitcases off the rack but a quarter of a mile away, was already feeling nervous and unhappy. He had never wanted to come because he detested the country and found himself completely out of place in the *Wise Owl* household. Sally was just the kind of girl he didn't like, for although she wasn't bad looking she never seemed to listen to what he had to say and had a nasty, hot temper. He had never found it easy to meet her grey eyes, either. Paul and Veronica were just kids and didn't count and he was scared of Uncle Wilfred, whom he could never understand.

61

Aunt Margaret had always been decent to him but there was a look of Sally about her and he knew that it would be very unwise to offend her. And, strange though it seems, he really did think there was something to be ashamed of in keeping a shop, and because of some equally unkind and snobbish thing he had once overheard his father say, he thought Uncle Wilfred was a failure just because he hadn't much money.

The train slowed down and he put on his school cap. It was pink with a design of an eagle on the front. Rather defiantly, he leaned out of the window, wondering whether Margaret would be there to meet him. Then he saw Sally, with a boy almost as tall standing beside her. She looked different out of London. She was bare-legged and wearing dark blue shorts and a bright yellow shirt open at the neck. Her face, legs and arms were very brown and her black hair, as he remembered it, was smooth and gleaming. As the train stopped she looked up, recognized him and nudged the boy at her side. If this was Paul he was certainly much bigger than he had expected.

While he was fumbling with the handle Sally stepped forward coolly and opened the door.

'Hullo, Tony. Is that luggage all yours? . . . Give a hand, Paul.'

Almost before he could move the two of them had his cases on the platform while he was left, feeling rather foolish, with two tennis rackets and a raincoat. Paul nodded 'Hullo' and suppressed a titter but refrained from asking him if he had his umbrella, and then, as the train puffed out, the three of them stood staring at each other in silence until Sally remembered her manners.

'I hope you had a pleasant journey,' she said politely. 'It's very hot isn't it?'

This was Tony's chance and he threw it away. If he had stuffed his cap in his pocket, grinned at them both and said, 'Decent of you to have me like this. I'm looking forward to you showing me round,' all would have been well.

But he didn't. He looked down his nose at them and said, 'Too hot to be standing about here. I s'pose we've got to walk with this luggage to your place, haven't we?'

Paul flushed.

'Our father,' he said, 'has arranged for a car. I've got the money. I expect he thought you'd be quite fagged out ... Please will you carry down these bags for us, Ernest?'

The porter winked at the Richardson children as he carried the cases down the steps to the car in the station yard.

'Nice day for holidays, Sally ... Catching many fish these days, young Paul?'

'You said you'd come with me one Sunday, Ernest. I'd like to come fishing with you. I bet you know the places. Shall we go when we come back from Wales?'

The old man heaved the cases on the front seat of the taxi and pushed his peaked cap to the back of his head.

'Aye,' he said. 'I'll come with you, lad. We'll pack up some food and drink and we'll have a rare fine day together ... Good day to you all.'

Tony sat forward uncomfortably and looked at Paul in astonishment. 'You're not really going fishing with him, are you? He's only a porter.'

'I bet he's a good one,' Paul flashed, 'and of course I want to go fishing with him. He knows more about the river than anyone round here. Besides he's a friend of ours. We've known him ever since we came here.'

After that the conversation languished although Sally did her best to be polite by pointing out some of Nettleford's landmarks.

'That's the church over there,' she remarked, rather obviously, 'and the big house behind the elm trees is the vicarage. We've got friends there and I expect you'll soon meet them ... And that's the *Horse and Groom* – it's got rather a jolly sign. '

Tony nodded gloomily and fidgeted with his cap.

'What's that on the front?' Paul said suddenly. 'It looks like a lobster to me.'

'You wouldn't know any better, of course. It's an eagle. My school is called "Eagle House".'

'Shucks!' Paul murmured and winked at his sister.

The car stopped at the *Wise Owl* and Wilfred came out to meet them.

'We're all glad to see you, my boy. Come upstairs. We have been waiting tea for you,' and Sally noticed that Tony made no attempt to carry either of his cases.

Margaret greeted him affectionately and for the first time since his arrival he managed a smile. Then Veronica shook hands with him solemnly, which seemed to surprise him almost as much as her, 'Thank you very much for coming to see us.'

As soon as his bedroom door had closed Paul turned to Sally.

'Everything you said about him is true – and worse. We'll have to stop him wearing that cap,' and then his father came in so they said no more.

There were cold sausages for tea and Tony enjoyed them. After his fourth he plunged into the conversation so suddenly that the others were stunned into silence.

'Seen any good films this week? I suppose you've got a flickhouse in this place?'

Wilfred winced and put down his fork.

'I beg your pardon, Tony. What did you say? What sort of house?'

'Flickhouse, Uncle. Place where you see the flicks. Cinema.'

'Thank you, my boy. Most extraordinary word. Yes, we have a cinema here, but I don't think any of us have been lately. We never go in the summer and are old-fashioned enough to prefer books in this house.'

'You miss a lot that way,' Tony replied. 'Often I don't have to read a book just because I've seen it on the flicks . . . Saves a lot of trouble.'

Margaret changed the subject hastily while her husband choked into his teacup, and then Veronica took a turn at keeping the conversation alive.

'Will you please tell me why you're wearing a suit like that and it's not Sunday? It looks very new doesn't it? You are smart.'

'Don't take any notice of her, Tony,' Margaret laughed. 'She admires you very much, but I hope you've brought some old clothes as well. You'll be out exploring a lot I expect, and Paul will certainly want to take you fishing.'

Paul flashed a glance at his mother which she pretended not to see.

'I shan't want to fish,' Tony said. 'Might play some tennis if there are any decent courts round here, but I didn't know what you do down here in the hols . . . What do you do, Sally?'

Sally was so surprised at being addressed direct that she dropped her knife with a clatter.

'Do? What do we do? . . . Well I s'pose we could play tennis if there are any strings left in my racket. There are two public courts, but Liza is better than me. I don't think much of tennis . . . What else do we do? I don't know how to explain. There's always something to do here. We help at home a bit and go and see our friends. Sometimes we go on bikes, and there's the farm at Northend. We'll take you there. It's a wonderful place, and I think we're going to be asked to help with the harvest soon. We've nearly always got something to do . . .'

'I can't see what,' Tony said. 'Seems pretty dull to me,' and when Sally looked at her mother she saw that her cheeks were very pink and her eyes bright with anger.

'Come down to the study, Sally,' her father said as he got up. 'I have something to show you.'

The empty shop was still warm and the light through the yellow blinds soft and mellow as she followed him over to his old roll-top desk. He put an arm round her shoulders and held her close.

'There are some new books today which you will like to see, Sally, but there is something I want to tell you first . . . This boy upstairs is unhappy. He does not realize how lonely he is. I know you do not like him. I know how difficult he will be, but I want you – if only for your mother's sake – to be friends with him and make him realize that this is the happiest home he has ever been in. You're old enough to understand that if you give the lead Paul will follow. Make it work, Sall,' and he dropped his arm and fumbled for his pipe.

Sally stared down the shop.

'You don't know how awful he is, Daddy. I've never told you. In London, just before I left, he sneered at you because you kept a shop . . . I smacked his face . . .'

Wilfred chuckled.

'I should imagine that surprised him.'

'But don't you *mind*, Daddy? Don't you feel insulted? Can't you see that he's felt snobbish about us ever since he arrived? He doesn't fit in here. He never will.'

'I'm not insulted, Sally. I'm proud of my job and of you, too, for standing up for me. You've got to make him fit in here. That's going to be your job these holidays. Quarrels are always a waste of time and there's good in everybody. You'll do it, won't you, darling? I'll be very proud of you if you manage it. Just remember that. "Daughters are the thing," as a character said in a play by the man who wrote *Peter Pan* . . . "Daughters are the thing".'

4

MAKING CAMP

NEXT morning when Sally was in the bathroom there came an agitated knocking on the door.

'Sally. Sally. Please come quick. It's the telephone with Aunt Mary an' I'm not sure what she said 'cos I hate the horrid thing, but I think she said that you must come.'

Veronica, clad only in her knickers and sandals, was prancing with excitement on the landing when Sally opened the door.

'I went to find the post. I want to do it one day by myself. Why shouldn't I do it, Sall? . . . But do please come now 'cos it's making noises.'

Mr Richardson had refused many times to have an extension of the telephone upstairs, maintaining that it had been installed for business purposes and that if people could not ring him up in business hours he did not intend to be disturbed in his home. At the same time he expressed himself strongly on the value of the written and printed word. His wife found his obstinacy in this respect very trying, and so, too, did Sally on this occasion as she tore down the narrow stairs with Veronica following more cautiously behind her.

The instrument was kept on her father's roll-top desk and when Sally, breathless but triumphant, grabbed it, it was still, as Vee had said, 'making noises'.

'Hullo,' she gasped, 'I'm sorry to keep you. This is the

Wise Owl, Nettleford. Richardson's Bookshop . . . Who is it, please?'

She held the receiver an inch or so away from her ear because the person at the other end seemed to be saying nothing but, 'Hullo, there. Hullo, there. Hullo. Hullo,' but suddenly this chanting ceased and a voice she recognized said, 'Good gracious, and who is that?'

'This is Sally Richardson. Is that you, Aunt Mary? Has something dreadful happened 'cos you're ringing up so early? Did you want Mummy?'

'Early, Sally? 'Tis after seven and we've been up here for hours. No need to call your mother now, my dear, if she's not downstairs. She can ring me later when you've talked it over.'

Sally's heart began to thump with suspense as she glared threateningly at Veronica who was standing on one leg beside her and trying to break into the conversation.

'What do you mean, Aunt Mary? Are you ready for us to come and help with the harvest? May we really come?'

'Now listen carefully, my dear. Talk this over with your mother and telephone me later. John says that this weather is going to hold for a few more days and that he must get everything in as soon as he can. Tell your mother that you and Paul and any of your friends who are ready to work can come over right away and help us . . . We thought maybe that if you could borrow one or two tents you'd like to make a camp and sleep out and cook your own food – that's really John's idea, o' course – what did you say, m'dear?'

'I didn't really say any word. I just gasped. I'm so excited I don't know what to say. It's wonderful. Of course

69

we'll come. We'll come today. Mummy won't mind . . . *Be quiet, Veronica* . . . I'll tell you in a minute . . . I'm sorry, Aunt Mary. That was Veronica interrupting.'

'And another thing, Sally my dear. I think your mother is looking very tired and although she told me that you're going away soon I'm sure she could do with a rest. Why don't you bring Veronica with you and I'll look after her? She'll sleep in the house, of course . . . If you can't get enough tents you girls could sleep in the barn even if you camped outside, but you'll have to let me know as soon as you can how many are coming.'

'It's a wonderful idea, Aunt Mary. I've never heard anything so marvellous, and thank you more than I can say for asking us. Do you mind how many people we bring, and what shall we do about food?'

'Telephone later about who is coming, Sally, and don't worry about food. Northend will feed its workers, John said, but you'll have to do most of your own cooking . . . Run off now and tell your mother that you'll all be welcome including my little love, Veronica . . . And you're all to wear your oldest clothes . . . Now I must go. Our love to you all.'

Slowly Sally replaced the receiver. Then, 'Did you hear that, Vee? We're all asked to Northend to make a camp and help with the harvest, and you're to come too if you like . . . Would you like to come?'

'Yes, I would, if you don't all interfere with me and make me do things I don't want . . . Will you sort the letters for Daddy now, Sall? . . . An' look. There's another letter just come through the letter-box . . . I'll get it.'

Surprisingly enough this was addressed to Sally. It bore

no stamp and was marked, 'PRIVATE' in large capital letters. She slit the envelope clumsily and took out a large sheet of paper covered with a jumble of words:

HAVE WE WANT ANY ICEBERGS TO FRIDAY AS KNOW US ALWAYS WHATS TODAY OR HAPPENED HAPPENING TO-MORROW HOW DO WE IS GO CINEMA TONY ALWAYS THE AND WE MUST HAVE KANGAROOS IF YOU OR ME ASKED BRUMAS YESTERDAY HIM OR HER TO HAVE KING JOIN SUEZ CANAL WHEN YOU ASK SHALL YOU OR WE HOPE ICES MEET ANYWAY HUGH LIZA STOP GO FIVE.

'Come on, Vee,' she said as she grabbed the little girl's hand, 'Come on and get dressed. You were very clever to answer the telephone. I'll tell Daddy you thought of the letters too . . . Bring them all and we'll sort them upstairs 'cos I'm in a hurry. You can bring down Phelpy's presently . . . Would you like to sleep in a tent at Northend or in the house with Aunt Mary?'

'With Aunt Mary,' Veronica puffed as she toiled up the steep stairs behind her sister. 'I like her. She'll read to me.'

'We'll ask Mummy at breakfast if you can go. Get dressed now, Vee, I want Paul.'

Veronica went obediently into their room while Sally flung open Paul's door. Then she stopped short in surprise. Her brother was standing in front of the open window, clad only in his pyjama trousers, with his arms raised above his head.

'What's the matter with you?' Sally began, and giggled when she saw the expression of surprise and disgust on his face. 'I believe you're doing *exercises*. Are you trying to make yourself a big, strong man?'

'You just mind your own business and get out of my room. Isn't there – any – any —'

'Privacy in this house,' Sally finished triumphantly for him. 'Look, Paul. I've got a code message which must be from Liza 'cos it's got her name in it, and Aunt Mary has just rung up to say we can go – as many as we like – to Northend today, if Mummy will let us, for the harvest an' she says if we could hire a tent or two we can camp out all the time and cook our food which she'll provide. What do you think of that?'

'Shucks!' Paul said as he subsided on to the bed and thoughtfully scratched one shoulder. 'Great suffering shucks. That's terrific . . . Now let's look at the code. I s'pose Liza got up early and shoved it in the letter-box . . . What was the key number? Three, o' course. Let's under-line every third word.'

That was soon done and the message came to life.

'Want to know what's happened how is Tony and have you asked him to join when shall we meet Liza five.'

'Five is the next key number of course. This is very bright of Liza. She's actually written it herself . . . I say, Paul. I'd forgotten all about Tony. What shall we do about him? Will he have to come to Northend with us?'

'You bet he will,' Paul said as he slipped his shirt over his head. 'Go away now and give me a little privacy in this house. Of course Mum will say "Yes", and I'll be on the tractor with Bill this afternoon if we're lucky. I like the tent idea . . . I s'pose we can ask Jimmy and Liza too . . . Now please go away. Go and wake up Tony. He hasn't got any sisters and you'll be able to have fun together.'

Sally slammed his door vigorously and went back to her own room.

Tony was late for breakfast but he did apologize.

'I couldn't get into the bathroom. There seemed to be somebody there all the time. I've got a wash basin with hot water in my room at home and I'm not used to this.'

'There's nearly always someone in *our* bathroom,' Sally said hotly, 'and we like it like that. It's more friendly. You'll have to be quicker in the morning or else we'll have to bring you your breakfast in bed ... Oh, all right, Mummy. I'm sorry if I was rude ... Sorry, Tony ... Mummy? May I give you a most exciting message from Aunt Mary now? It's very important.'

'Vee was trying to tell me something about it but I couldn't quite understand. I thought she said she was going to camp but sleeping with Aunt Mary, which didn't sound possible to me ... Tell me the worst, darling.'

Wilfred put down his paper and took off his spectacles.

'Many things seem to have been going on very early this morning. What is all this about the Northend folk, Sally?'

It didn't take long to explain and when she had finished she turned to Tony impetuously.

'You'd like to come, wouldn't you, Tony? Northend is marvellous. You've no idea what fun we have there.'

There was a long silence while their visitor reddened and looked down at his plate.

'Who else is coming?' he said at last. 'What would we have to do?'

'You would have to help in the fields as the others will help,' Wilfred said quite sharply. 'No doubt you'd have to do as you were told while you were working, and I guess

that the job John wants you all for is stooking – standing
up the tied bundles of corn in fours or sixes to dry in the
sun – and later on I expect you'd have to help with the
carting. You wouldn't be asked to do anything that Sally
and Paul don't do ... And why do you ask who else is
going?'

Tony still declined to meet their eyes.

'I didn't know I was coming here to work,' he muttered,
'and I only wondered if you and Aunt Margeret were
coming too. Any grown-ups, I meant.'

Wilfred looked as if he was going to lose his temper, but
Margaret knew all the signs and broke in quickly.

'No. There won't be any grown-ups, Tony, except our
friends, Mr and Mrs Wilkins, and the men who work for
them. As for what you call "working", I never heard such
nonsense. Once you've got there you'll thoroughly enjoy
yourself, and if I hadn't got to look after my old man here
I'd come with you ... Yes, my poppet, of course you can
go with the others if Aunt Mary has said she'll look after
you. I don't really see why you shouldn't sleep with Sall in
a tent if you want to.'

'I do,' Sally said quickly. 'There's lots of reasons,
Mummy. Will you ring up Aunt Mary and tell her it's all
right?'

'Who else are you taking? The vicarage children, I suppose?'

'I'll ask Elizabeth, of course. She'll love it. Mrs Langton
won't let Hugh come I'm sure, and Charles doesn't come
home until today with a friend.'

'We'll ask Jimmy Brand,' Paul said. 'I'll go at once and
ask him.'

'Could we go today, Mummy?' Sally pleaded. 'This afternoon, just as soon as we can get ready? Could we? The best part of doing something marvellous like this is to do it at once.'

'Of course you can, Sally. I often feel just like that and if Uncle John wants your help you might as well go as soon as you can. You'd better go to the vicarage first and see if Liza can come, and then we'll go shopping together ... And take Tony with you and cheer him up ... You stay and help me, Veronica. We'll do some women's work together.'

'Am I to have no say in all this?' Wilfred protested. 'No! Of course I am not ... Good luck to you all, anyhow. I wish I was coming with you.'

He got up, kissed Sally on the top of her head and went to the door.

Margaret and Veronica followed him out and the children were left alone. Sally and Paul looked at each other meaningly and then at Tony who was standing awkwardly by the window. Suddenly Sally was sorry for him, realizing that he was no more than a spoiled and lonely boy who was feeling miserably shy.

'Why don't you stop playing the giddy goat, Tony?' she said impetuously. 'We don't mind being friends if you'll stop being stuck-up and superior. Come round to the vicarage now and meet Liza and the others.'

'I've got to write a letter first,' he muttered. 'I shall see this kid presently I suppose if she's coming to the farm too? I'll stay here.'

Paul stalked across the room and flung open the door.

'Come on, Sall. You're wasting your time and breath. I wonder what his little fellow Eagles think of him?'

He turned and thrust out his chin belligerently in Tony's direction.

'You're bigger'n me but I'd like to bash your nose in. Any time you like, too.'

Tony, white-faced but for a patch of scarlet on his cheek-bones, stood where he was as the door slammed. Three minutes later when his aunt came back into the room he was still standing, miserably alone, by the window watching Paul and Sally running down the street.

'I'd like to write Liza a letter in code but we haven't got time,' Sally puffed. 'You nip in and see Jimmy right away and then come along to the vicarage – or if we're ready first we'll come back to Brand's. Cheerio.'

Paul dived into the gloomy doorway of the ironmonger's and Sally ran on.

It was going to be very hot again. If only they could borrow two tents she and Liza could share one and Paul and Jimmy the other. But what about Tony? He was going to spoil everything of course. How could they be friends with him? If he'd been decent just now she had been going to ask him to join the Owlers, but he was hope-less. He'd have to come with them, though, and that would mean another tent unless she and Liza slept in the barn. But what about *rats*? Surely there are always rats in barns? But would Aunt Mary have suggested a barn with rats in it?

'Good gracious, child, where are you going?' came a friendly voice as she banged into something soft and black which proved to be the vicar.

'I'm *so* sorry,' Sally gasped. 'I was thinking and didn't notice you, Mr Langton. How awful of me! I'm coming to

76

see Elizabeth so may I come with you? We've been invited to help with the harvest at Northend. We're going to make a camp. May she come with us, please?'

'You'd better come and have breakfast with us, Sally,' the vicar said as he fell into step beside her.

'But I've had one, thank you.'

'Come and have another. We like our friends to come to breakfast. I've just been to church and I need one.'

'Thank you very much but I only need Elizabeth. May she come with us, please?'

'I'm sure she can, but we shall have to ask her mother. I wish I was coming with you, Sally.'

Before Sally could agree or disagree Jimmy Brand came tearing out of the vicarage drive and brought himself to a sliding stop in front of them. Sally was certain that he would have passed them both at full speed if he had dared.

'Good morning, sir,' he gasped, giving Sally a horrible wink at the same time. 'Hullo, Sall.'

'Good morning to you, Brand. Can you tell me why you are rushing in and out of my house at such a speed and so early in the morning? Has anything serious happened? Perhaps you had better come to breakfast too?'

'Thank you very much, sir, but no thank you,' Jimmy said. 'Must be getting back now. Cheerio, sir.'

'Extraordinary boy, Sally . . . I wonder what he's been up to?'

Sally wondered too but thought he had probably been early at work with a match-box, a pulley and a thread, but all she said was, 'We all like Jimmy Brand very much. He's a special friend of Paul's . . . Look. There's Elizabeth. May I run on and tell her the news?'

Fortunately Elizabeth had had her breakfast and when she had recovered from the surprise of seeing Sally arriving with her father they went together under the cedar tree. Almost before Sally had finished her story Paul and Jimmy arrived.

'All right for me,' the latter said as he flopped down on the grass beside the girls. 'Paul told me. I can come. Dad says he wishes he was coming too.'

'Everybody says that,' Sally agreed. 'We've got to be careful to keep this to ourselves. You'd better go and ask right away, Liza. Your father said you could come – I asked him for you.'

Liza was back in three minutes.

'I don't think Mother really understands that I'm going to be away at nights but Father is a pet over this sort of thing. Anyway it's all right and I'm coming. I didn't ask about Hugh. He's too small even if Vee is coming.'

'What about Charles and his friend?' Sally said. 'Will they want to come? They might be very useful.'

'We couldn't ask them to be Owlers,' Elizabeth said. 'I'm sure Charles would say that was just a kid's idea. He puts stuff on his hair now and I don't know this other boy he's bringing home today. They could always come over on bikes and help couldn't they, even if they don't camp with us. What about your little Tony?'

Sally's face fell.

'He's hopeless. We tried to be decent to him but it won't work, but he's coming with us. We can't leave him behind.'

'He's scared of coming. That's the trouble,' Paul said. 'He's a sissy and he tries to be a bully. We'll have to put up with him.'

78

'Why?' asked Jimmy.

'Because he's our cousin, I s'pose,' Sally said. 'We're very, very sorry about him but our parents have said we've got to look after him.'

'We don't have to make him an Owler, do we?'

'Of course not, Jimmy. I nearly asked him this morning, just because I thought it might cheer him up, but I didn't . . . We'll never ask him unless he does something decent and sensible. We do hope you won't be too mad with us because of him. I promise Vee won't be any trouble.'

Liza and Jimmy made appropriate and embarrassed noises to show that they understood the unfortunate position in which their friends were placed and then the vicar, wreathed in clouds of tobacco smoke, strolled across the lawn.

'Just had an idea,' he beamed at them. 'Two wonderful ideas. If you're going to camp you want a tent. Fellow I know called Jones – used to be our scoutmaster – has got one and he'll lend it to you. I've just telephoned him. He calls it a "Half Patrol" and says it will sleep three at a squeeze . . . Says he can lend you ground-sheets, too . . . How many of you going?'

'Jimmy, Paul and our cousin, Tony, who came to stay with us yesterday, Liza and me to begin with,' Sally said. 'Vee is coming too, but she'll sleep in the house with Mrs Wilkins . . . And thank you about the tent. That's marvellous. If there's only one, Liza and me could sleep in a barn – or the boys could take it in turns. I don't see why the girls should have rats all the time.'

'What's the other idea, Dad?' Liza said as she got up and

stretched. 'This is such a beautiful morning for us that I feel anything might happen now.'

'I thought I'd take you all over in the car,' the vicar smiled. 'Save a lot of time and bother if we do it that way and no doubt you'll have plenty of gear to take with you . . . Now, I don't want to organize you but you boys had better go and see Jones about the tent while the girls get together on the other odds and ends. Let me know what time you'll be ready to go this afternoon,' and he wandered back to the house.

'Meet here in two hours,' Elizabeth said, 'although I don't know what I shall do in all that time. Maybe I'll come with you, Sall. I expect we'll have to do some shopping. Will your mother help?'

'Of course she will. She's wonderful over this sort of thing.'

'My mother is wonderful,' Liza sighed, 'but *not* over this sort of thing . . . I'd like to come with you.'

'Just a sec.,' Jimmy said, looking a little redder than usual. 'What about this gadget I'm fixing for you? I made the pulley and I got a little tin and I run back for some fishing line and the bell. Aren't we going to do any more 'bout it, or have I been wasting my time? . . . Just tell me that.'

He looked so aggrieved that neither of the girls dared to laugh at him although Paul did.

'Silly ass! Of course we'll use it when we come back. Let's go and see Jones. Camp is what matters now!'

The girls went back to the *Wise Owl*.

'It's all fixed, Daddy. Liza and Jimmy are coming with us and we've got a tent for three and the vicar is going to

take us over in his car this afternoon. Please may I telephone to Aunt Mary?'

Wilfred nodded and shook hands with Elizabeth.

'A pleasure to see you again, my dear . . . And now
you're going off again to Northend? Good! We shall try
and come over and see you . . . This fine weather is not
much good for book-selling.'

Sally came back from the office with a radiant face.

'It's all right. Aunt Mary is marvellous. And it isn't a
barn we can sleep in but an old granary without any
grain, up in the roof of the biggest barn and she says she
doesn't know what a rat is . . . Where's Tony, Daddy?
Paul and I tried to be friendly with him after breakfast
but it won't work. I suppose he must come with us? You
and Mummy wouldn't care to have him here on your
own, would you?'

Wilfred shook his head.

'I think that is his trouble, Sally. He prefers grown-ups
to children of his own age. Perhaps Elizabeth can persuade
him to change his mind.'

And the strange thing was that Elizabeth certainly did
succeed in making him a little more human and perhaps
this was because she had never met him before and was
not the sort of girl to stand any nonsense. She was indo-
lent in many ways but as she walked up the stairs behind
her friend she made up her mind that it was silly for any
boy to upset two nice people like Sally and Paul and that
she would try and do something about it. They found
Tony sitting at one end of the kitchen table peeling
potatoes with Veronica opposite to him shelling peas.
Margaret was busy between them writing a shopping list

and as Sally rushed at her to tell her the news Elizabeth caught Tony's embarrassed eye and smiled at him. He didn't look too bad. A bit scared and much too tidy in his London clothes.

'Hullo, Mrs Richardson,' she said. 'It's grand to be home again and wonderful of you all to ask me to North-end. We hoped that you would help us do some shopping because we don't know much about camps . . . Hullo, Vee! My father says you're a poppet! Are you?'

'I am, and I'm coming to the farm with you and I can do what I like.'

Then Elizabeth turned to the embarrassed potato peeler. 'You must be Tony. I'm Elizabeth Langton but you can just call me Liza like all my other friends. I'm glad you're coming with us. Boys are useful in camps I believe. They do everything except the cooking.' She sat on the edge of the table. 'You're doing those jolly well, isn't he, Mrs Richardson? I never peel potatoes if I can help it – I'd rather eat them with the skins on – but when I do, there never seems much potato left after I've finished with them. Your job in camp is fixed for you, Tony.'

And Tony actually laughed.

'Now we'd better make a list for you campers,' Margaret said, 'and we shall have to hurry if you're going after lunch. Have any of you ever done this before?'

Tony and Sally shook their heads.

'I've slept in a tent in the garden,' Elizabeth said, 'and Charles and me used to make fires and cook potatoes, but I don't think that's proper camping. I believe Jimmy is the expert.'

'It doesn't seem very long ago that I went camping,'

Margaret said as she sucked the point of her pencil and looked rather like a naughty little girl. 'I think I can remember what you'll want . . . Tony! Tear a sheet off that writing-pad on the dresser and make a list as we go. If these other scatterbrains have got any sense they'll make you Quartermaster . . . And I hope you've got a proper pencil!'

Tony had a beautiful propelling pencil and seemed quite pleased to be given a definite job.

'You'll all be responsible for your own washing things,' Margaret began, 'and remember to keep them separate. I must find you a towel each. Write Towels in capital letters, Tony. Then there's blankets, because I don't suppose any of you have got sleeping-bags. You'll want two each and we can manage that. We haven't got ground-sheets but perhaps Jimmy and Paul will get those from the useful Mr Jones. Now clothes. You girls ought to wear dungarees: if you haven't got them I should buy them now. You'll get scratched to bits stooking . . . Vee's got some dungarees so she'll be all right even if she's only feeding the ducks . . . I know Aunt Mary says she'll feed you but you must take some stores and some tinned things and I'll buy those for you . . . Matches and candles, Tony, but better than candles a hurricane lamp. I expect there are plenty at the farm but you'd better take two in case. If you girls are going to sleep in a granary you mustn't have a naked flame. Crockery? I suppose Aunt Mary will supply that, but I'll ring her up and ask. You must take two billy-cans, a big kettle, and a frying-pan. You'll have to do your own washing-up so you must have scrubbing brushes and drying-up cloths. Put those down, Mr Quartermaster . . . You're not camping properly, of course, because you're sure to be fairly near the house and that will save you a lot of trouble. If Aunt Mary will allow you it would be best to keep all your food in her larder so that you're not bothered with flies. Be sure to take a chopper and perhaps a small saw for firewood, and if Jimmy really does know about camping he'll know how to make a fire . . . Tea, coffee and cocoa, Tony. I'll supply that and of course Mrs Brand will let us have some for Jimmy. That's another thing you'll have to remember, Tony – your list will have to be passed on to Paul and Jimmy . . . You'd better take some first aid things. Aspirins, liver pills, Vaseline, bandages, lint, iodine, anti-midge lotion and something to help if you burn or scald yourselves, which you probably will . . . Finished, Tony? Good . . . Now shall we all go out together and buy what we need or would Elizabeth like to go back and see what she's got at home first? Why don't you take Tony with you, Liza, and if you meet Paul and Jimmy tell them what's happened and we'll all meet later at the *Hobby Horse* for ices.'

And that was what they did. Tony handed over his list, after making a few independent notes on another sheet of paper, and went off with Elizabeth, who gave Sally a wicked wink over her shoulder.

'Well!' Sally said when they had gone. 'Only about an hour ago he told me that he'd meet her soon enough and wouldn't come out with me when I asked him. What's come over him?'

'Somebody is taking the right sort of notice of him,' her mother said. 'I like Elizabeth. I think she'll be very good for Tony.'

The shopping did not take so very long. The shops were close together in Nettleford and when they called into Brand's, Jimmy's father was already getting together some very useful gadgets for campers, including two shining billy-cans, a frying-pan, a special tin-opener and a hank of rope.

'Yes, Mrs Richardson,' he said. 'We've heard all about it and very glad we are for Jimmy to get a break like this. The two of 'em have gone off to find Jones now, but if he hasn't got ground-sheets I can lend them. Good morning to you, Veronica. I hear you are going to Northend too.'

'Good morning, Mr Brand. I like the smell of your shop very much. It's quite special.'

Mr Brand liked praise so while Margaret was upstairs discussing rations for Jimmy with his wife he presented Veronica with a set of miniature clothes pegs just in case she wanted to do any of her own washing while she was away.

They left a message for the boys to meet at the *Hobby Horse* and then went on to the draper's for dungarees for Sally. Here they found Tony standing solitary and disconsolate with a shopping basket outside the shop.

'Don't laugh at him,' Margaret whispered as they came up. Then, 'You don't seem to be wasting much time, Mr Quartermaster. I congratulate you if you've managed to organize Elizabeth. She's the untidiest young woman I know. Where is she?'

'In here buying things, Aunt Margaret. I don't like shops like this.'

Margaret stopped on the step and looked at her nephew thoughtfully.

'Have you brought any old clothes, Tony? *Really* old clothes I mean – corduroys and sports shirts and a sweater?'

He shook his head.

'Have you got much money, Tony? Enough to buy yourself some camping clothes?'

'I think so, but —'

'No buts, Mr Quartermaster. You come in here with us and when we've finished with the girls we'll send them packing and do a little shopping for you.'

Sally couldn't help laughing at the expression on his face, but when he managed a smile in return she felt that they were getting on.

Half an hour later they met the boys in the *Hobby Horse* and when Paul saw Tony with a large parcel he raised his eyebrows. Sally shook her head warningly but Paul was even more astonished when his cousin turned to him, and with a rather sheepish grin, said, 'I've been getting some camping clothes. Is the tent O.K.?'

'Yes,' Paul replied hurriedly. 'Yes, that's O.K. Oh, yes . . .' and then, remembering his manners and forgetting that not long ago he had offered to bash Tony's nose in, he added, 'This is Jimmy Brand, who's coming with us.'

Jimmy, now half-way through a double strawberry ice, nodded briefly.

'We gotta tent. That's O.K. I know all about tents and can fix it. You don't have to worry about that, Tony.'

'Of course it's nothing to do with me,' Margaret said as she rummaged in her bag for some change, 'but if I were you I'd make Tony your Quartermaster. He's been making notes all the morning and I know he's good at lists. With Elizabeth and Sally in the party you'll want somebody who is a good organizer.'

A long silence was broken by Veronica.

'What is a Quarmasser? Nobody tells me anything.'

'Looks after the stores,' Jimmy replied, and then added rather half-heartedly, 'Jolly good idea, Mrs Richardson. Every camp has to have a Q.M. and if Tony will do it that's fine . . . You'd better come back to my place now, Tony, and get our stuff together and check it on the list.'

Both Paul and Sally seemed so dazed by the turn of events that neither had any alternative suggestions to make when Elizabeth said, 'I think we ought to put everything that we've got to take on the vicarage lawn before lunch so that Dad can see the worst before he starts. It's not fair to expect him to go to three different houses collecting stuff like a jumble sale . . . I'm quite sure we'll never all get in the car as well. I think Sally and Paul and Jimmy and me ought to go on bikes. Tony and Vee can go with Dad.'

Veronica looked at Tony under her lashes, and then, a little doubtfully, at her mother who nodded. Events were moving out of her control, but as she liked the vicar this plan was probably as good as any. She did not care for cycling.

The rest of the morning passed quickly enough as the pile of suitcases, haversacks, tins, blankets and baskets on the vicarage lawn grew like a Guy Fawkes bonfire before November. Tony, still in his flannel suit and with the perspiration running down his pale face, worked like a beaver while Elizabeth lay in the shade of the cedar and encouraged him.

87

'Who's going to do the cooking?' Jimmy called as he staggered up with a green canvas bucket filled with crockery.

'Sally and me, I s'pose,' Liza replied. 'I can only hope that Sall is asking her father to lend her a book on camp cooking. You boys will have to take it in turns to wash up . . . I s'pose you're going to check all this in at the other end, Tony? . . . It's lucky my brother and his friend don't turn up till this afternoon. What would they think if they saw this lot? . . . Would any of you boys like to pump up my bike tyres?' She lay back luxuriously and looked up at the blue sky between the branches of the cedar. 'Boys,' she mused, 'are the most selfish and thoughtless of all God's creatures . . . '

'We'll be ready about half-past one,' Paul called from the gate. 'Tell your Dad we'll help pack everything in before we start on our bikes.'

What the vicar said when he came home for his lunch and saw the pile on his lawn is not recorded, but when Elizabeth noticed the expression on his face she hastened to assure him that he would only have two passengers, and as one of them would be Veronica the back of the car should be able to take everything else.

'Indeed I hope so, Elizabeth. Those on bicycles will be safer.'

Before the vicarage lunch was over Paul and Jimmy arrived and when they were given permission began to pack the car. So well did they do it that Mr Langton had little to suggest when he came out and inspected the result of their work.

'Difficult to recognize my car, boys. You'll have to cycle

hard behind me in case something falls off . . . Ah! Here is
Sally with my poppet . . . And the young man? . . . How
do you do, Tony? You, I understand, are to be my
passenger with Veronica.'

Tony was dressed now in his new country clothes –
brown corduroy shorts, grey shirt open at the neck, and
shiny brown sandals. His bare knees and his neck were
very white, and although he did not look as miserable as a
few hours ago he was obviously still very shy. He shook
hands with the vicar, avoided Elizabeth's welcoming grin
and then snapped at Paul.

'You might have waited until I'd checked everything
on my list. I'm responsible if I'm the Quartermaster,
aren't I?'

'We couldn't wait while you were changing, Tony.
Jimmy and me got on with the job. You can see there's
nothing left on the grass so it must all be in . . . You'd
better get in yourself and cross yourself off your list.'

The vicar looked at Paul over the top of his glasses, but
the boy seemed quite unperturbed. Certainly these
youngsters were very outspoken these days!

Suddenly Veronica flung her arms round Sally as if she
was never going to see her again.

'Come quick as quick, Sall. We'll be waiting for you all.
Give Mummy and Daddy my love.'

The vicar squeezed into the driving seat, Tony got in
the other side and pulled Veronica on to his knee. The
others, with Mrs Langton now behind them in the porch,
waved and cheered as the laden car scrunched up the
drive.

The journey was uneventful except for the creaks and

groans of the tortured springs of the car and Veronica's frenzied cries of 'Faster, faster!' as they rushed down the hill after leaving the beech trees behind.

When they pulled up outside the farmhouse Mrs Wilkins was in her garden, but Veronica was out of the car and through the gate almost before she recognized them.

'I'm the first, Aunt Mary! This is the vicar and you know him, and the boy is Tony, our cousin, who is *very* shy. The others are coming on bikes.'

'Come, Tony,' the vicar said as he got out. 'Come and meet your hostess.'

Mrs Wilkins shook hands with Mr Langton who was an old friend, and looked Tony up and down with shrewd but kindly eyes.

'Pleased to have you here, lad. Looks as if some country air will do you good and there's plenty of work to do I promise you . . . The first ricks are going up in the yard and John's cutting as hard as he can . . . There's stooking enough for twenty of you . . . Sit down in the shade, Vicar, and wait for the other youngsters. Veronica, my love. Take your cousin and show him the farm. The car can be unloaded when the others arrive.'

'I'll show you my ducks,' Veronica said, and to Tony's astonishment took his hand and led him into the lane down which was coming a great, red tractor, belching blue fumes and hauling a farm cart loaded with golden grain. The brown-faced man on the driving seat waved cheerfully to Veronica, who yelled, 'Hullo, Bill. We've come to stay. We've come to make a camp and help you all.' But whether or not Bill heard what she said he kissed his hand to her as he swung his load through the farmyard gate. Veronica, pulling Tony behind her, followed him into the rickyard beyond. Here was another cart with a horse between the shafts standing before a half-made rick and Tony, feeling rather shy and foolish with little Veronica as his only guide, watched the two men on the cart spearing the sheaves with pitchforks and tossing them up to two more men above them on the rick.

'Now I'll show you my ducks and a bull in a shed and the cows . . . No! I can't show you the cows indoors yet 'cos it's too early for them to be milked . . . Come and see my ducks, Tony. They stand on their heads.'

She led him into a field surrounded with noble elm trees, in the far corner of which was the pond. Cows were in this field and Tony did not care for them, but as Veronica did not seem to mind them there wasn't very much he could do to show his distaste. He had never really considered ducks before and was finding them as fascinating as did his cousin when a yell from the direction of the farm announced the arrival of the others.

After that Tony passed through the most confusing and exciting three hours he could remember. Mrs Wilkins told them first that her husband was cutting a field about a mile away and would not be back for hours, but that they were to start their camp at once. Then she led them across the lane to a field opposite the house.

'Anywhere here you like,' she said, 'and if I were you I'd keep fairly near the gate to save you walking too far. You can use the house for bathroom and larder which will save you trouble as you'll be working a lot o' the time, but the stream runs down the side of the field . . . Vicar says you've only one tent to sleep the three boys so you'd better store what you don't want in the barn under the granary where the girls will sleep . . . If you get to work now I'll have tea ready for you on the lawn in two hours, but you'll have to cook your own supper . . . I'll see you girls after tea about provisions . . . Let me know if there's anything you want.'

Mr Langton then backed the car into the field. The sun was very hot and although he took off his coat and repeatedly removed his spectacles and polished them, he worked harder even than Paul, who dashed to and fro like a little terrier.

'Choose your camp site carefully,' the vicar panted. 'Not under the trees. Never under trees and particularly never under elms, whose branches often break off without warning . . . It should be under the hedge but near the stream . . . What about the tent? Have you found a level pitch, Jimmy? Good. I'll help Paul get the tent up and you can begin on the fireplace . . . Tony! If you're Quartermaster you'd better help the girls unpack and store stuff you don't want at once in the barn.'

Paul lent a willing hand with the tent and Jimmy certainly knew about camp fires. While the tent was going up, the latter, with his big sheath knife, cut out a square of turf about three yards from the tent site and moved it, rolled up like a Swiss roll, to the hedge. Then he ran into the farmyard and rummaged round until he found some bricks. These he placed on the bare patch of earth in two rows about a foot apart at the windward end and six inches at the other so that the draught would draw the flames and heat up to the billy-can or frying-pan resting on them at the narrow end.

Meanwhile, Tony and the girls were unpacking and when the axe was found Paul took Vee and disappeared up the hill towards the wood. He did not make the mistake of picking dead wood from the hedges because Uncle John had once told him that it was placed there to keep animals from breaking through. When they came back half an hour later, dragging a bundle of kindling and bigger wood behind them, the tent was up and the blankets were hanging on a line between two posts in the sun.

'We've unpacked,' a red-faced Tony said as Paul came up. 'Anything I can do to help you? I reckon I know where everything is.'

'We'll have to chop up this if we want a meal tonight,' Paul said, 'but let's have a drink first. Vee. You're Aunt Mary's pet. Run over and see if tea is ready . . . Just look at the vicar, Tony. I often wondered if he wore braces. He does. They're black.'

The sound of a bell came from the garden across the lane and very thankfully the boys and Mr Langton went over.

'You all look very hot,' Elizabeth said rather obviously as she came out of the house carrying a tray. 'Sall and me like our granary very much. We've got it beautifully tidy.'

'You've had nothing to do with it then,' Paul said as he flopped down into the shade.

'Oh yes I have. And we've got some hay to put our ground-sheets on and there's a window at the end, rather like that one in our attic, and we can both look out across the farmyard right into the camp . . . Come and see it, Daddy, won't you, before you go.'

Mrs Wilkins now appeared with two enormous teapots

and nearly dropped them when she saw the vicar in his braces prostrate in a deck-chair.

'Forgive me rising,' he puffed. 'I am incapable of movement for at least ten minutes . . . I should be in my parish I know, but the tent is up and I think these young-sters will manage now . . . What do you say, Brand? Is there anything else I can do for you?'

Jimmy, with his mouth full of bread and butter, shook his head solemnly.

'No, thank you, sir. I don't reckon there is. Will you come and help us take it down?' and the wink which he gave to the rest of the Owlers caused Sally to choke into her teacup.

They waved the good-natured man off after tea and then trooped into the farm kitchen to help wash up. Then Mrs Wilkins took Elizabeth off and showed her where she had put stores for the campers to use, while Sally took the boys into the big barn which seemed almost as lofty as a cathedral except at the end above the big double doors. There was a fixed ladder in the corner and this led up into the granary. 'It's not used now, Aunt Mary says,' Sally explained, 'but they used to store the grain in these partitions. They make fine bedrooms for Liza and me, but if we get tired of sleeping in here, you boys will have to change.'

'You girls like attics, don't you?' Paul said as he wrinkled his nose. 'I can't think what it is I can smell up here, but I'm sure it's something old. Maybe you'll have found out by the morning . . . Come on. Let's go and find Uncle John.'

Veronica decided that she had wasted too much time

already and went to the duck pond, but the others, directed by the men still working in the rickyard, found the farmer in a field nearly a mile away. He was driving a tractor himself and waved when he saw them at the gate. Behind the tractor was the machine called the binder with a big, wooden-bladed wheel beating down the standing grain on to its hidden knives and then flinging out the tied sheaves on the other side. He was cutting the last few yards, and panic-stricken rabbits were running in all directions. With a whoop of joy Jimmy dashed into the field and flung himself without success at one of them. In the far corner some boys and women were stooking – lifting the cut sheaves and standing them upright in pairs on the stubble so that the tops were close together. Each stook was made of six sheaves with three on each side.

'That's what we ought to be doing,' Elizabeth said, 'but we'll start early tomorrow.'

Mr Wilkins jumped off the tractor and felt for his pipe as Sally led the race across the stubble to greet him. He shook hands with them and to Tony's surprise spoke to him just as warmly as he did to the others.

'Fred over there'll bring the tractor down,' he said. 'We'll walk down together and I can stretch my legs. You'll stook this field tomorrow. How are they getting on in the rickyard, Paul?'

'Nearly finished the second, I think, Uncle John. They look fine.'

'Good. It's not such a bad harvest, but this weather can't last for ever . . . Have you brought young Vee?'

The sun was lower as they walked down the hill towards the clustered roofs of Northend and a welcome little

96

breeze just stirred the tree-tops. The hedges smelled of honeysuckle and the air throbbed gently with the sound of the tractors in the rickyard, and Tony, as he strode along between Paul and Elizabeth, wondered whether he was dreaming.

Mr Wilkins approved the camp site, wished them luck and went over to see how his precious ricks were progressing, leaving the Owlers and Tony to prepare for supper.

Considering everything it was a good supper. Paul prepared a fire which would have roasted an ox and certainly singed his eyebrows when he got the wrong side of it. Elizabeth and Sally put too much fat in the frying-pan and set it alight, but at last, when the sun was sinking in a blaze of glory and the bats were fluttering over the farmyard in the scented dusk, they settled down at a respectable distance from the fire and enjoyed a mighty meal of sausages, well-fried bread, eggs and tea. Veronica, who had refused point-blank to go to bed at her proper time, found her portion too much for her and dozed against her sister's shoulder. Elizabeth yawned as if she would never stop and Tony, still in a daze, was sure he had never felt so tired. Only Jimmy passed his plate for a second helping and went on chattering as if the day was only just beginning.

Then Mrs Wilkins came across the road.

'My little love,' she crooned as she lifted Veronica into her arms, 'and here have I been forgetting all about you and these stupid ones doing nothing about it.'

'I'm not sleepy,' Veronica murmured. 'Not very and I like camping very much . . . Goo' ni', Sall . . . Goo' ni', Paul . . .'

Mrs Wilkins stood above them with the glow of the fire lighting up her kindly face.

'You're enjoying yourselves, I hope,' she smiled, 'but 'tis time you turned in. John will light a lantern for you girls when you come to say "Good night" . . . And Good night to you boys. You'll sleep well I'll be bound.'

They called 'Good night' to her and then Elizabeth said, 'We ought to sing songs round the camp fire but I just can't. Let's leave the washing-up until the morning . . . Can you boys manage if we go now? I'm so tired I can hardly get up . . . Come on, Sall.'

'No need to go yet,' Jimmy said. 'I reckon this is the best time of all. Camp fires are grand. Only trouble with this one is that it was too hot. Paul will do better tomorrow.'

'I'll wash up in the stream,' Tony said unexpectedly. 'I don't mind. We can't start tomorrow with dirty plates.'

'Can't we?' Elizabeth yawned. 'I know we shouldn't, but can't we? It's jolly decent of you, Tony, anyway, and I'm sorry that I just can't help you . . . Good night, chaps! . . .'

Sally stood up. 'Thanks, Tony,' she said shyly. 'I do hope you like Northend. Come and wake us in the morning if you're up first . . . Good night all . . .'

The two girls walked slowly across the road.

'I can't see much wrong with your Tony,' Elizabeth said. 'He just wants bringing out a bit.'

'Maybe he does, Liza. You seem to be doing it . . . Maybe Daddy was right about him. He generally is.'

'What did he say?'

'I'll tell you in the morning. It would take too long now.'

They went into the big kitchen where Mr Wilkins was dozing in his chair and his wife was busy with her knitting.

'The little lamb was asleep while I took the clothes off her,' she said. 'Here's your lantern and some matches if you want them in the night, but you won't, for the moon is up in an hour. God bless you both.'

She kissed them both and Mr Wilkins roused himself sufficiently to do the same and then, hand in hand because the farmyard was dark and rather eerie, the two girls went over to the barn and up the ladder to their strange bedroom.

'I'm too tired to clean my teeth,' Liza yawned, 'but I'll scrub them twice as hard in the morning.'

They scrambled out of their clothes and into their pyjamas and said their prayers – not very long prayers, perhaps, but very heartfelt. Elizabeth adjusted the cushion Mrs Wilkins had given her for a pillow and rolled herself in a blanket and then tucked the other round her feet.

'Buck up, Sall,' she whispered. 'This is heavenly and the hay smells wonderful.'

But Sally was still kneeling by the window. The rim of a great, golden moon was just showing above the wooded hill-side. A white owl sailed silently over the roof of the house and she could just hear the voices of the boys in the field over the lane. And as she watched she saw a little square of yellow light in the darkness below and knew that they had lit their lantern in the tent.

She sighed happily. It had been a wonderful day.

5

FIRE!

As soon as the girls had gone Tony began to pack up the dirty plates. He wished now that he hadn't promised to wash up because what he really wanted to do was to go to bed – any sort of bed, anywhere. His face and his bare arms and knees were throbbing with sunburn and he was so sleepy that he staggered a little when he moved across to Jimmy who was now lying full-length on the grass watching the dying embers of the fire.

Then Paul stood up and stretched.

'This is all right,' he yawned. 'This has been what I call a jolly decent sort of day. I hate the idea, Jimmy, but we've got to help Tony . . . Come on.'

'Those girls,' Jimmy said as he got up, 'aren't too bad. Your sister is not too bad at all, Paul. She cooked those ausages jolly well. I like 'em hard outside.'

'Elizabeth is all right, too,' Tony muttered.

'I never thought girls would be any good on a show like this,' Jimmy went on, 'but I'd like to have a shot at cooking one day and let them do the washing-up . . . What do we do with all this grease on the plates? Wipe it on the grass?'

'It would be better to wipe them with a bit of newspaper and burn the paper,' Paul said, 'but don't let's do that now. Bring them over to the stream.'

'I'm going to light the lantern in the tent and see what it looks like,' Jimmy said. 'I'll come over in a sec. Honest I will.'

Paul, with his arms full of dirty crockery, ambled over to the stream just behind his cousin.

'You ever done anything like this before, Tony?'

'You know I haven't.'

'D'you like it? I mean, we were worried about you coming and we thought maybe you wouldn't like anything we did.'

Tony turned and waited for him.

'I didn't think I'd like it, but this camp is fine . . . Let's wipe the plates on the grass first and then swish 'em about in the water.'

The stream ran along the side of the meadow under a hedge. It was not really big enough for bathing, but it was a foot deep in the middle and ran strong and clear through a culvert under the road to feed Veronica's duck pond before meandering on down the valley.

Tony knelt on the bank. The grass was cool and refreshing to his knees as he plunged his hands into the water.

'It's cold!' he gasped. 'Gosh, it's cold! I'm going to shove my head in.'

Jimmy came up then and found the water just as inviting, and it was ten minutes before they all ran back with crockery which was wet if not very clean.

The moon was up now and their little tent glowed with an amber light in the dusk.

'We'll never all get in there at the same time,' Paul said.

'There's hardly room for us to sleep, anyway. I'm going to undress by the fire.'

'Don't leave your clothes or your shoes outside or they'll be soaked with dew in the morning,' Jimmy warned. 'I'm going to make a pillow of mine. We'd better get in the tent one by one and I'll show you how to roll yourself in one blanket and tuck it round your feet . . . Come on, Tony. You first.'

Tony never realized just exactly what Jimmy did to make him so snug and it was several nights before Paul and he learned to get themselves into two blankets as well as he did. But although it hadn't seemed possible, it wasn't long before all three were actually ready for sleep in this one small tent.

'Goo' ni',' Paul yawned. 'I'm blowing out the lamp but I've got a torch in my shoe here. Goo' ni' both.'

'You O.K., Tony?' Jimmy whispered. 'It'll seem awful hard at first but you soon get used to it . . . Thanks for being Quartermaster. We haven't lost a thing yet . . . 'Night.'

The tent door was open and Tony, from where he lay enveloped like a Red Indian's papoose in his blankets, could see the outline of a great elm tree against a star-spangled sky. The top of the tree was strangely silvered in the light of the moon he could not see, but as he watched the stars multiplied, twinkled, went out and then seemed to pop up again somewhere near. It was almost as if the sky was alive.

A big bird drifted soundlessly across the tent opening and suddenly the silence was shattered with a long drawn-out, eerie cry that made his scalp tingle. Paul, on one side, grunted and Jimmy whispered, 'Owl. I bet he's got a nest in the barn. You'll hear his mate call soon . . . You don't snore, do you, Tony?'

'I don't think so. Do you?'

'No. Baby owls do though. If we could get near that

nest we'd hear 'em making most 'straordinary row . . .
Goo' ni' . . . ' and his sleepy voice trailed off into silence.

But sleep would not come to Tony. The ground under
the thickness of his two blankets and ground-sheet was
very hard. His pillow, which was a rucksack stuffed with
some clean shirts, was uncomfortable and the night was
now alive with strange noises. The tent wall, a few inches
from his ear, creaked in a gentle breeze; the owl called
again from much farther away; there were mysterious
rustlings from the field outside and, when all else was
still, he could hear the murmur of the brook. More of the
tree now was touched with a silver radiance and, as he
watched, the moonlight began to creep across the strip
of grass which he could see through the open door of the
tent. Both his companions were asleep and Jimmy was
purring gently at his side.

Tony thought of them at home in the big flat high
above Regent's Park. Of his father, always too busy to
understand what he would like to do and nearly always
suggesting the things which seemed to set him apart from
most of the other boys. Of his mother, who gave him what
he wanted if it could be bought, but who always seemed
to be having parties and doing things which were con-
cerned with his father's business.

He had hated the idea of coming to the *Wise Owl* – of
being pushed off to relations who lived an entirely different life and who, he was sure, didn't like him. Besides,
there was Sally. He didn't know much about girls but he
was scared of her. He was never likely to forget how she
had slapped his face and her habit of staring at you with
those big, grey eyes so that you didn't know where to

look. But perhaps she wasn't so bad after all – although very different from Elizabeth who, he was sure, would never slap anybody's face and had behaved just as if they had known each other all their lives. It wouldn't be too bad if they had, Tony thought. He wouldn't have minded a brother – and a sister, too, for that matter. Paul seemed all right, now they'd got down here, although he'd been rather touchy this morning. He was much bigger than he'd expected, but the odd thing was that none of them seemed to want to have a row, and although he knew he looked a bit peculiar in his new country clothes, none of them had laughed at him although they knew quite well how awkward he was feeling.

It had been decent of Aunt Margaret to suggest him being Quartermaster, and Uncle Wilfred had not been too bad, either, although he'd been a bit touchy about the flicks. Funny how easily people got upset about something quite ordinary! Funny, too, how a man who was so crazy about books would get so excited about working on a farm . . .

Tony stretched his tired limbs and suddenly longed for his soft bed at home – or even the bed on which he had slept at the *Wise Owl*. Anything would be better than this. He'd never sleep a wink. Then he realized that although the fresh air about his face was refreshingly cool his body was warm and that it was possible to get comfortable in a different sort of way.

The owl cried again and then came a strange whirring noise which Elizabeth told him one day must have been a nightjar.

Although the air in the little tent was fresh Tony began

to wish that he was outside. Then he felt that if he turned over he would disturb the other two and suddenly there was nothing he wanted to do more than to turn over. He wriggled and squirmed until he was on his other side and the other two slept on peacefully. He wondered then if he could crawl right out of the blanket, step over Jimmy and go out on to the moonlit meadow. He was too hot . . . the grass would be cool . . . but not as cool as the water of the brook . . . Somebody had once said that water sang as it moved over stones and it was true . . . this brook was singing . . . he could hear it now . . .

Tony slept at last. Perhaps it was because he had more on his mind than the other two or perhaps it was because the wind rose during the early hours of the night, but he woke again quite suddenly when the luminous hands of his wrist-watch showed five past three. Paul and Jimmy were still breathing quietly and all was quiet except for the creaking of the canvas of the tent and the sound of the wind. The moon was high and outside all was nearly as clear as day.

He was beautifully warm and not too stiff, but his heart was thumping uncomfortably. He raised his head and listened, but except for the wind there were no other sounds, for now he could not even hear the water. But somehow he was uneasy and felt sure that something had wakened him. Very gently he sat up and strained his ears again. No. Just the wind which was blowing quite strongly now from the direction of the farm and buffeting the tent behind him. Then his nose told him something else. There was a slight smell of burning – probably wood smoke. He sniffed again. There was no doubt of it. Probably the rising wind was fanning the embers of the big fire which Paul had built and which they had not troubled to stamp out? But of course that couldn't do any harm even if the wood flared up again, so Tony pulled his blanket up to his chin and lay down once more.

The smell was quite strong now. Was it wood? Suddenly he was sure that he must put his mind at rest. He must go and see if the camp fire was all right and he must go without the others knowing, because he would certainly look a fool if he woke them and they asked him what he was doing. Perhaps a spark might blow against the tent or set the dry grass of the field alight? It was dry enough to burn for it hadn't rained for weeks . . . That was the smell, of course. Burning grass. Not wood.

He wriggled out of his blanket, crawled over Jimmy and out of the tent into the moonlight. The trampled grass was cool to his bare feet and the wind ruffled his hair as he looked round. The smell of smoke was quite strong but when he glanced at their fire he saw at once that there was no life left in those embers. He ran across and poked the ashes with a stick but they were grey and dead.

He stood up and looked over the road to the farmhouse and the barns. All was quiet. The windows gleamed coldly in the moonlight and the shadows at the side of the house were heavy and black in contrast. He glanced up at the chimneys but no tell-tale wisp of smoke from them gave him the answer he wanted.

Another gust of wind stirred the tree-tops, struck chill through his thin pyjamas and brought with it the unmistakable smell of burning. There *was* a fire somewhere.

Perhaps on the other side of the barns which he could not see from here?

Tony, forgetting himself and his own troubles for the first time for many months, clutched at his pyjamas and ran for the gate into the lane. He was barefooted and unused to taking much exercise but he half-tumbled, half vaulted over the gate just to save himself the trouble of unlatching it. He turned to the left and raced up the road towards the farmyard and as he did so he heard, for the first time, the dread crackle of fire.

He was fighting for breath now, and as he fumbled with the catch on the farmyard gate he wondered whether he ought to raise the alarm at the house first? But perhaps it wasn't anything much after all? He slowed down through the farmyard because he was out of breath and a cruel stitch was stabbing at his side. His right foot hurt, too, and he was sure it was cut and bleeding. He glanced up at the window of the granary where the girls were sleeping and then stumbled on into the rickyard where the men had been working this afternoon.

One of the two new ricks close to the barn was alight down the side facing the wind. Sparks and smoke were flying up and when a fresh gust came the burning straw glowed red and hungrily.

'Fire!' Tony yelled instinctively, and then turned to run back and raise the alarm. As he did so he saw a shadowy form racing down the side of the hedge that divided the rickyard from the lane.

'Hi!' he shouted. 'Hi, you! Fire!'

But the man – if it was a man? – raced on, crouching low and not even turning his head as Tony shouted again, and then disappeared into the shadows under a clump of elm trees in the far corner of the rickyard.

A glance over his shoulder showed Tony that the flames were creeping up the rick. He tried to raise a shout as he ran back across the farmyard to the house but when he got to the front door all that he could do was to lean against it, sobbing for breath, and bang on it with his clenched fists. Then he pulled himself together and found the knocker and an old-fashioned bell-handle. He pounded on one and tugged at the other until a bell began to ring wildly inside the house.

'Fire!' he yelled again as his breath came back. 'Mr Wilkins! Get up! Please hear me!'

A window above his head opened with a crash.

'Who's that?' came the farmer's voice. 'What's wrong?'

'It's me. Tony. Your ricks are on fire. I've just seen a man running away . . . What shall I do?'

'Wake the others, lad. One of you run up and wake old Tom. I'll telephone for fire-brigade. We'll be down. Get some clothes on and get busy.'

Tony found himself doing what he was told without argument. Nothing like this had ever happened to him before and as he ran back towards the tent he couldn't help being rather glad that this was something which he had done without the others either helping or patronizing him.

Jimmy was crawling out of the tent as he came up.

'What's up? What's all the row? What are you doing?'

'Fire, Jimmy! The ricks are on fire – I've given the alarm. We've got to find Tom and wake him. Who is Tom? D'you know?'

Jimmy turned round and grabbed Paul's feet.

'Get up!' he yelled. 'The farm's on fire. We've got to help. Who's Tom?'

Paul was the least excited of the three. He yawned, stretched and began to pull his shorts on over his pyjama trousers.

'Give me my shoes and my clothes,' Tony snapped. 'We've got to hurry. Who's Tom? We've got to wake him.'

Paul began to throw articles of clothing out of the tent rather like a terrier scratching out earth between his hind legs.

'What did you say was alight?' he said. 'One of the ricks? Shucks! Do you think my camp fire did that?'

'Who's Tom?' Tony shouted. 'We've got to find him.'

'Old Tom? I know him,' Paul muttered through the folds of his sweater as he pulled it over his head. 'I'll find him. He lives in the cottage up the hill,' and without further argument he slipped on his gym shoes and raced across the field.

Over the road a door slammed and Mr Wilkins shouted, 'Come on, boys. We'll try buckets from the horse-trough.'

Jimmy and Tony, very oddly dressed, ran to join him in the farmyard. The smell of smoke was very strong now and as they came in at the gate the farmer was hurrying across from one of the barns with four buckets clattering.

'Start filling 'em from the trough,' he gasped. 'I'll go and see what the trouble is. Fire-brigade's on the way, I hope.'

'Paul's gone for Tom,' Jimmy shouted as the farmer ran for the rickyard. 'Where are you going, Tony?'

Tony was pushing open the doors of the big barn.

'We've forgotten the girls. I'll get 'em up,' but he had barely got his foot on the ladder to the granary when Sally's head appeared out of the shadows above him.

'What's happening? What's all the row about?'

'Ricks on fire. Buck up and come down. We've got to fill buckets.'

Elizabeth's fair head gleamed pale beside her friend's.

'Oh, Tony,' she said. 'How wonderful. You've rescued us from an awful fate.'

It was impossible at the time, and difficult later, to piece together the events of the next half-hour. Tony remembered Mr Wilkins running back into the farmyard and snatching two brimming buckets which neither he nor Jimmy could even lift.

'Might be worse,' he gasped. 'We'll get it out if the wind doesn't rise, and the men get here quick.'

Then the girls appeared.

'We'll fill the buckets,' Sally snapped. 'You boys carry one at a time between you to Uncle John. Where's Paul?'

They explained, and soon after the young man himself trotted calmly into the farmyard.

'Tom's coming! He be cursin' and swearin' something awful but he be coming ... Shucks! What a do! ... What do you want me to do? Carry a bucket on my head? Where's the fire anyway?'

Mrs Wilkins, disguised in an old raincoat, soft felt hat and rubber boots, next rushed into the farmyard like a whirlwind.

'Rakes and forks!' she gasped. 'That's what we want. Pull the rick to pieces ... Good! Here's Tom ... Come

on, Tom. Not the first time we've been in a mess together.'

Tom looked a fearsome sight too but he didn't
waste any words and by the time the fire-brigade arrived
the fire was out and the second rick and the barns were
saved.

The firemen ran their hoses to the pond and pumped
water over the smoking straw scattered about the rickyard
and sprayed the roofs and wooden walls of the barns while
the children, black-faced, dishevelled, dressed in each
other's shorts and sweaters and with the legs of their
pyjamas soaking wet, gathered round admiringly.

As the sky in the east lightened and the stars began to
fade Mary Wilkins went over to her husband who was
leaning on a pitchfork and said, 'Seems as if we've got to
be grateful to our young friends this night, John. Who was
it gave the alarm?'

Sally, standing next to Tony, whose mother would
certainly never have recognized him, pushed her cousin
forward.

'It was Tony, Jimmy says. He's the hero. He rescued us
girls, too. Nobody had thought about us in the granary,
but you were all making such a row that we couldn't have
slept through it even if we wanted to . . . Aunt Mary! I've
just had an awful thought. Veronica! What's happened to
her?'

'God bless the child!' Mrs Wilkins said, 'and may I be
forgiven but I'd forgotten all about the precious lamb . . .
Come now with me, Sally, and see if she's all right and
then you can help me get some tea ready for us all.'

'I'll come too,' Elizabeth said. 'I'd like to get into

some of my own clothes before I appear at a party, even if it's only a fire-party. Sall's shorts are a bit tight for me.'

Veronica was still sleeping when Sally crept up the stairs and peeped into her room, but she could not help wondering what her determined young sister would say when she found out what had been happening during the night and what excitement she had missed.

Half an hour later, just when a new day was beginning, all the fire-fighters met in the kitchen. Mrs Wilkins had found time to make herself look what she called 'respectable', while Sally and Elizabeth were now dressed in their own clothes and had washed their faces at the sink and tried to tidy their hair. Tom came in with four firemen. He had worn his old hat throughout the proceedings – Paul told them all later that he was sure he must sleep in it – and as none of the children had ever before seen him without it they were thrilled, when he removed it in deference to Mrs Wilkins, to see that he had iron-grey, curly hair.

'Isn't he sweet?' Liza whispered to Sally. 'Quite distinguished.'

The three boys had made no attempt to clean themselves. Tony, it is true, would have liked to have done so, but as neither Jimmy nor Paul seemed to think it mattered he thought it better not to make such a suggestion. Twenty-four hours ago he would have sneered at them for being content to look like gutter-snipes, but the Tony who now flopped into a chair, pushed back his lanky hair with a filthy hand and then grinned, almost shyly at Sally, was already a very different boy from the unhappy prig who arrived at Nettleford, defiant and bitter, such a short time ago.

Mrs Wilkins poured the tea into thick mugs which Elizabeth handed round, and when her husband had taken a deep draught he stood up in front of the fire and smiled round upon his friends.

'I want to thank you all,' he began, 'and specially our young friends here. Tom, of course, I thank, but he and I have worked together many a year and we know each other's minds and what we think o' the other. But you youngsters have done a fine job and we'd have been in a poor way without you . . . Now young Tony here, who's never been on a farm in his life afore and never slept out of an ordinary bed till tonight, is the one who was smart enough to smell smoke and do something about it. He hasn't told me much but I do know that he ran to the rickyard to make sure something was wrong before rousing me, and we're still wondering why young Veronica didn't hear him. He's told me enough, too, to make sure enough that this fire wasn't an accident for he did see someone running off in the dark out o' the rickyard . . . But that's another matter I'm to be seeing about for I've an idea who it may be. All the same it's a good thing to keep a cool head and not shirk your duty, and it's a better thing still when you're in a strange place among those you don't really know well, and that's why I say we'll drink a health in Mrs Wilkins's tea to young Tony here!'

And so they did while Tony, not knowing what was expected of him, just went scarlet in the face and muttered, 'It wasn't anything. I woke up and smelled the smoke. I haven't done anything.'

Then the firemen got up to go because, as they said,
'You never know when there's going to be another fire,'
and Paul slapped Tony on the back so that he choked into
his cup.

'Oh boy!' he said. 'If your mother could only see you
now . . . Did you wear your eagle cap to the fire?'

And the strange thing was that Tony laughed as loudly
as the others while the grown-ups looked on astonished.

'You'll do no stooking today,' John Wilkins said when
he had seen the firemen off. 'Not unless you want to o'
course. You'd better be going back to bed.'

They laughed at him and told him that was nonsense
and then Mrs Wilkins invited them to breakfast indoors.

'Thanks all the same, Aunt Mary,' Sally said, 'but
we'd rather keep on with our cooking practice outside.
We're going to have porridge this morning and then
scrambled eggs. Don't think we're rude when we say "No
thank you," will you?'

'You can do what you like, my dear, but one thing I'll
insist on. Before you do anything else those three boys are
to go up to the bathroom and scrub themselves decent.'

The boys went up meekly enough and when they were
clean they all walked over the road to the tent together.
The grass was thick with dew, the wind had dropped and
a little mist lay over the road and down by the stream in
the low-lying parts of the meadow.

'Better start our fire I s'pose,' Tony said. 'Shall I do it
or will you, Paul?'

He was walking a few steps in front and did not see
Paul grimace at the others who all nodded violently.

'We all ought to know about fires by now,' he said, 'and

you more than any of us. You have a go at laying and lighting it this morning.'

Then he nodded at Sally, who went rather pink and said, 'There's something we wanted to ask you, Tony. Just before you came down here we started a secret Club – sort of secret society – with just us four as members. We've got a code and although we're very new we wondered if you'd like to join . . . You don't have to *do* anything special except just be a member . . . We'd all like it if you would join. Will you?'

Tony, who was bending over the pile of kindling when she began to speak, turned round and goggled at them while Sally was making her little speech.

'Me?' he said after a long silence. 'Do you really mean you'd all like me to join up with you in something? . . . A secret Club did you say?'

'We did,' Liza laughed. 'Of course we want you and you can't jolly well stay out now 'cos we've told you too much.'

'Thanks,' Tony said. 'Thanks very much. I'd like that.'

'That's another thing settled then,' Paul grinned. 'I reckon we'll call you "Big Chief Eagle".'

6

OWLERS TO THE RESCUE

THE Owlers enjoyed their lunch under a hedge in one of the last fields to be carried. Not until they had been working for an hour that morning did the farmer tell them that this was the last day and that they would celebrate with a Harvest Home Supper in the big barn tonight.

'You'll all be welcome,' he twinkled, 'and I told Mrs Wilkins to ring your father and mother, Sally, and ask them to come over this afternoon just to see how you're all behaving yourselves and to stay on for the jollification . . . When you go down for the basket presently, you might remind her and if she hasn't had time to telephone maybe you'd like to do it yourself.'

Sally and Paul went down together and found Mrs Wilkins and some helpers cleaning out the barn. Aunt Mary had forgotten to telephone, so Sally had a happy ten minutes talking to her mother. They promised to come over in the afternoon and have tea with the campers and stay for the supper, and Sally and Paul carried the basket up the hill again and then decided, with the others, to break camp the next day.

When they arrived Mr and Mrs Richardson inspected the camp and seemed delighted with everything they saw. Soon it was tea-time   .

'You mustn't mind the tea tasting a bit of wood smoke, Dad,' Paul said as he passed his father a large mug. 'We've got used to it now though we shall never get used to the girls' porridge . . . How do you think we're all looking?'

'Wonderfully well, Paul, all of you.'

'And now,' said Margaret half an hour later, 'you girls had better come indoors with me and see if we can help Aunt Mary. I've brought your frocks, too, when I heard there was going to be a party.'

But the girls were fetched out by Uncle John ten minutes later so that they all, with Veronica seated on the neck of Primrose the old cart-horse, could ride into the rickyard on the last load.

Wilfred stood by the gate as the cart lumbered in. John Wilkins pushed his hat back and wiped his forehead. 'Harvest home,' he said, 'and thank God for it.'

Never had the children seen such a feast as that laid for them all in the great barn that night. The table was loaded with bread and pies and cold chicken and cheese and jam and honey and cups and glasses. There was a barrel of beer and a barrel of cider, and only an hour before they had all trooped in, Mary Wilkins had remembered that somewhere in the attic were paper chains, and Sally and Elizabeth had found them and fixed them up. Two hanging oil-lamps and the coloured lanterns lit the gay scene.

Veronica had been put to bed for two hours and looked the better for it. The boys had done their best to smarten up, while Sally and Elizabeth, in their party frocks, were the success of the evening. All the farm men and their wives and sweethearts were there with John Wilkins at one end of the table and his wife at the other. Sally found herself next to a shining-faced Bill and was introduced to his wife as 'This is young Sall, Molly,' and Molly said 'Pleased to meet you.'

Just before they sat down a slim, dark man slipped into the barn and went up to Mr Wilkins.

Veronica, who was holding her uncle's hand, heard him say, 'You'd better sit next to this young lady, with Tom t'other side. It's up to you, Harry. Tom knows. I'll tell the others,' and then to one or two near him he said, 'Young Harry's back with us. He made a mistake and so did I and that's all there is to it. He's right worried about his missus in hospital.'

Later, when the table was bare, they all sang songs, many of which the children had never heard. They drank toasts too – the first for the Queen, and then Mr Wilkins thanked everyone who had helped him; next Bill proposed Mrs Wilkins's health, and finally old Tom held his mug high and called out in a loud voice, 'Good luck to the young 'uns, sez I, for they've worked right well.'

But all good things come to an end, and at last Margaret, who had not enjoyed an evening so much for years, got up and said that they must go.

'Come and sleep in our granary, Mummy. Don't go yet,' Sally pleaded, and Jimmy added, 'I don't know if we could squeeze Mr Richardson in our tent, but if we did his feet would be outside it.'

Wilfred reminded them of the *Wise Owl* in the morning and said that they intended to walk up to the main road and then catch the last bus to Nettleford.

'And even if we miss the bus we shall enjoy the walk,' he persisted, when Mr Wilkins said he would run them home

in the car. 'This is a night to remember and these youngsters will walk up the hill with us.'

'We can't go to bed until they've finished down here anyway,' Sally said. 'If we went up now we'd be suffocated with tobacco smoke. We'll all walk up with you.'

At the top of the hill, where the beech trees began, they said 'Good night'.

'You've been away long enough,' Margaret said. 'Come home tomorrow. The vicar says he'll fetch your luggage and there's plenty to do at home . . . Will you be ready to come, Tony?'

Tony's face was in shadow as he answered.

'If the others want to, Aunt Margaret. Whatever they want to do I'll like.'

As soon as the Owlers came home the weather broke in a succession of thunderstorms.

Elizabeth tried to organize an early meeting of the Club so that Tony could be properly enrolled, but Paul and Jimmy both made it clear that they preferred fishing in the rain to a crowd in a stuffy attic, so that as soon as the formalities were over the party broke up in disorder.

At the *Wise Owl* Tony now found himself accepted as one of the family. Nobody reminded him of his previous behaviour and once Paul actually asked him if he would like to come down to the river and pick up a few hints, and although he was relieved when Tony declined, the invitation had been sincere.

There was much talk about the coming holiday at Tenby and almost every time Wilfred came up from the shop he brought a fresh book on South Wales and a different map which they all studied together.

And then came the morning when Wilfred ran upstairs

at ten minutes past nine, opened the door of the kitchen where they were all helping to wash up and announced:

'Phelpy isn't here.'

Nobody took any notice except Veronica, who was sitting on the table singing and swinging her legs, and all that she said was, 'It isn't dinner-time yet. Why have you come back, Daddy?'

'PHELPY HASN'T ARRIVED!' he shouted, so loudly that Tony dropped a plate and caught it just before it hit the floor. 'Will you all please stop this noise and pay attention?'

Order was restored and Margaret said, 'I expect she's arrived by now, darling. Don't look so worried.'

'But she's never been late before. She's always there. She has her own key. It is most inconvenient when she does not come.'

And then it occurred to them all that Phelpy was the sort of person who was rather like a piece of furniture which stays where it is put.

'She might be ill,' Margaret suggested, 'but I'm sure that if she is she'll let us know. You'd better go back, Wilfred, and see if there are any customers or whether the telephone is ringing.'

'I'll come with you,' Sally volunteered. 'The others can finish drying up.'

But when they went down there was no familiar Miss Phelps flicking the bookshelves with a feather duster.

'I think you'd better run round and see if she's coming, Sally. Will you do that for me?'

'Of course. Where does she live?'

'How should I know, my dear? She's never told me. It

121

is most extraordinary but we know next to nothing about her.'

'But you must have her address written down some-where, Daddy. Paul followed her home once, because she's so mysterious, to that road by the gas-works, but I don't suppose he'd remember which house . . . Look in her office, Daddy, and see if her address is on something.'

Wilfred did as he was told and proudly produced an insurance card.

'There you are. Phelps, Gertrude Amelia. 9, Artillery Road, Nettleford . . . I wish you would run along, Sall, and see what's happened.'

'I'll go on my bike. Shan't be long.'

Artillery Road was a depressing, dead-end road which hardly seemed to belong to Nettleford, beyond the railway station.

There were twelve semi-detached villas on each side of it and above the front door of each was an oblong of glass on which was painted, in grotesque lettering, a name. Sally knew enough geography to guess that the builder must once have lived in the Isle of Wight, for the first four were called, 'Shanklin', 'Sandown', 'Cowes Villa', and 'Newport House'. Number Nine, which had its number painted on the gate, was named in the same tradition, but quite inaccurately, 'Seaview'.

Sally leaned her cycle against the fence and pushed open an iron gate which squeaked. The path to the front door was of black and white tiles and a neat little plot of soil in front of the window was gay with scarlet and yellow nasturtiums. She tried to peep into the front rooms with-out success, and then rang the bell. After a minute or so she heard a strange tapping and then the door was opened by a grey-haired woman who looked at her in surprise.

'I'm sorry to bother you,' Sally said breathlessly, 'but please does Miss Phelps live here?'

'I am Miss Phelps.'

'You're not the one I mean. I'm sorry if that sounds rude. I want the Miss Phelps who works at the *Wise Owl*. She didn't come this morning.'

The woman smiled faintly.

'You must be Sally. Gertrude has often told me about you. I am her sister and I think you had better come in.'

Then Sally noticed that this Miss Phelps was a cripple who limped even with the help of a stick. She led her to a sitting-room at the end of the hall and as soon as she pushed back the door Sally saw a wheeled chair.

'I am very glad you have come, my dear,' she said, 'because my sister has been worrying that she has not been able to telephone your father. I find it difficult to go very far myself.'

'I am so sorry. I do hope our Miss Phelps isn't ill?'

The grey-haired woman sat down in the wheeled chair and pulled it round so that she was facing Sally. She looked worried and almost ill herself and her knuckles were white as she gripped the arms of the chair.

'My sister has lumbago. In spite of all her efforts she could not get out of bed this morning. I do not remember her being unwell for many years and it is most difficult for me to get upstairs to her . . . Our neighbours would have helped but are away on holiday. I wonder if you would leave a note for the doctor when you go back, Sally?'

'Of course I will, and I'll explain everything to my father. Is there anything else I can do now? . . . P'raps I could go upstairs and see her?'

She didn't particularly want to do this but she did feel sorry for them and was also rather curious. If she could see Phelpy in bed in her own room she would certainly have something to tell Paul.

'Do, my dear! The room facing the top of the stairs. I'm sure she will be pleased to see you.'

Sally ran and knocked timidly on the door before she could change her mind.

'Who is that?' boomed a familiar voice.

'It's me. Sally. May I come in?'

The first thing she noticed when she closed the door was that the room was surprisingly bright and cheerful and glowing with sunshine. The walls were primrose and above a long, low, white shelf of books on the wall opposite the window several coloured pictures hung in a row. Gay curtains were fluttering gently in the breeze. By the bed was a table with a vase of summer flowers and in the bed, propped up with pillows, was the surprising vision of Phelpy, with her sandy hair looking quite fluffy, her spectacles slightly askew and wearing a bright green bed-jacket.

They stared at each other for almost a minute of silence, both trying to get used to an unusual situation.

Then, 'I hope you didn't mind me coming up, Phelpy,' – the nickname slipped out unawares and neither of them noticed it – 'but Daddy sent me to see if you were coming and then Miss Phelps downstairs said about your lumbago and I wondered if there was anything I could do.'

'Very kind of you, Sally. Very kind. I would like you to leave this note at the doctor's and explain to Mr Richardson how humiliated and ashamed I am to be so helpless. I shall resume my duties just as —'

'Of course you will,' Sally interrupted. 'Would you like a cup of tea, or what we call a "hottie", in our family?'

'A hottie?'

'Hot water-bottle.'

'I would appreciate both very much. My sister, Mabel, will tell you where we keep the – er – hotties ... Sally, child' – she tried to raise herself and winced with the pain – 'I think I must explain that my sister must not wait upon me. She is not strong enough to do so. I must get well soon because there is no one else to look after my sister properly. She cannot come up to me, you see, and sleeps in the front room downstairs. Please take this note to the doctor's as soon as you can ... You are a thoughtful child, Sally ... Do you like my room?'

'I do – very much. It's a lovely room. Much nicer than —'

'You'd imagine from the look of the outside,' Phelpy smiled. 'Yes, I know, Sally. Artillery Road is not very beautiful. I do my best with my room.'

'I'll light the gas under the kettle and rush up on my bike with the note and make the tea and fill the bottle when I come back.'

As she was picking up the envelope from the table she could not help seeing a coloured card with the message 'Many Happy Returns', and at that very second she had her brilliant idea.

'I shan't be long,' she smiled from the door and said the

same to sister Mabel downstairs as soon as she had found the kitchen and the gas stove. 'I'm just going to the doctor's but don't you move if the kettle boils over. I'll soon be back . . . 'Bye.'

She was back in ten minutes.

'He's still doing his surgery but they say he'll come as soon as he can.'

She made the tea and filled the bottle and took them both upstairs.

'I don't want you to worry any more, Phelpy. The doctor will soon make your back better and I'll come with someone and cook your lunch. We'd love to do that. Just you explain it to us and your sister needn't worry either. I'll explain everything to Daddy. Goodbye for the present,' and she ran out and closed the door before Phelpy could answer.

Miss Phelps downstairs admitted that today was indeed her sister's birthday.

'I guessed it was. I believe she wants cheering up and I've got an idea that we'd like to give her a birthday party. Don't you think it would do her good?'

Miss Phelps senior became very agitated.

'But my dear child, I know that you're very kind and thoughtful, but I'm sure the doctor would never allow such a thing and besides, we could not have any party here . . . I cannot move about very much and you could hardly hold it in Gertrude's room —'

'I don't see why not and we could help you up too . . . I don't mean a *wild* party you know. Just a birthday tea and a cake and p'raps some paper chains and some music —'

'Stop, child! What you say is quite impossible. I am

grateful for your help now, but we do not know what the doctor will say.'

'All right, Miss Phelps, but if he comes this morning we can ask him. I'm coming back soon with a friend who's a good cook and we'll get lunch for you and then there'll still be plenty of time to talk about the party. Don't you worry. We'll manage everything,' and she ran out for her bicycle, leaving the bewildered lady with a look of horror on her face as she pictured the Phelps homestead overrun with noisy strangers giving her sister a party that she might not want.

When Sally got back to the *Wise Owl* her father was struggling with two large parcels and looked up hopefully at the sound of her step. She told him the news.

'Of course we'll do all we can to help you, Daddy, and although I love it down here I think I shall have to go to Artillery Road today. I promised to cook their lunch for them – Elizabeth will help I know – and I'll tell you another thing I've found out! It's Phelpy's birthday and I've seen her in bed and if she's better I've got an idea that we could all give her a party!'

Wilfred dropped the parcel.

'*All* give her a party? Nonsense, Sally. I shouldn't dream of going and I'm sure your mother wouldn't do so either. If you can help her now, do so by all means, but surely if she's well enough for a party, she's well enough to be here.'

'We can give her a party in bed, but we'll only do it if the doctor says so,' and Sally ran upstairs to find the others.

She told her mother first.

'Of course you can go and help if they want you, but

don't give them camp cooking! Is her sister really an invalid, Sall?'

'She's got a wheeled chair but I don't know whether she can get upstairs.'

'I wonder why Phelpy has never told us about her? I suppose she comes out to work so that they can live together. But how does she manage as she's away all day?'

Sally explained about the neighbours who were now on holiday and rushed up to find Paul and Tony who were fiddling with one of the former's relics in his room. Paul was particularly impressed with her news.

'You actually went into the house and saw old Phelpy in bed? Had she got paper cuffs on? What did she look like?'

'Not a bit the same. Nicer . . . sort of wistful. No cuffs.'

'Wistful? What's happened to you, Sall?'

She told them her plan.

'You don't seriously mean that you and Liza are going up there to *cook* for them? And Phelpy is ill already? It might be murder. We must tell the police, Tony.'

'But there's something for the Owlers to do. This is our big chance. We can't all go and cook but we could give her a birthday party in her room to cheer her up. We'll make a cake —'

Tony groaned and hid his face in his hands.

'Yes we will, and stop being so funny both of you. You're the only ones to laugh at your own jokes . . . If the doctor says it can't hurt her it's just the sort of thing we ought to do. Will you go and ask Jimmy if he'll join in, and we'll meet after lunch and decide what to do . . . I'm going to find Liza.'

She met her friend coming out of the chemist's shop.

'Of course I'll come. I've finished the shopping but I must tell the parents that I'm off on a mission of mercy. They will be pleased with you for thinking of it, Sall. I'll come on my bike, and of course the party idea is wonderful. I don't see how lumbago could stop a party, do you? I've never had it but I must admit that father has more than once, and when that happens I keep out of the way because he's so bad-tempered.'

A quarter of an hour later they met the doctor coming out of Number Nine, Artillery Road.

'Hullo, Sally. I heard you were coming back here. And how's Elizabeth? Have you two really come to help?'

'Yes, we have. Is Phelpy better? We want to give her a party. It's her birthday.'

The doctor leaned against the gate and looked at them.

'You're serious about wanting to help? These two old dears need it, you know. The elder one is nearly helpless and yours won't be much good for a few days. I've lent her an electric pad for her back and we'll send her some medicine and she must be kept warm.'

'Yes, we'll help. We can do shopping and cooking. Can she eat anything and can we give her a birthday party?'

'She cannot eat anything – light diet, please – and I think that perhaps what she needs more than anything else is to realize that somebody else is thinking about *her* instead of her doing all the thinking for other people ... But the party must be a *quiet* party. How many are coming?'

Sally hesitated. 'Three boys and us and perhaps Veronica. It sounds a lot but I promise that all we'll do is just to cheer her up and we will be quiet.'

'Very well. No more than an hour.'

'Can the other one get upstairs, doctor? We ought to give it for them both.'

'Yes, if she's helped. It won't hurt her . . . Now I must be off. Do what you can, girls. Goodbye.'

They rang the bell and Miss Mabel opened the door.

'It is kind of you to come. I hope you have explained to your father, Sally? My sister is more comfortable now, so perhaps you would like to go up and see her . . . Surely you are the vicar's daughter, my dear?'

'Yes, I'm Elizabeth. What would you like us to do first? We met the doctor outside and he says "light diet". Would you like to risk omelettes? . . . You go up and see your Miss Phelps, Sall, while I'm talking things over with this one – and don't tell her about the party.'

Very few people were able to resist Elizabeth when she made up her mind to be pleasant and Miss Mabel was soon overwhelmed by her.

'You don't have to worry any more at all,' she began. 'Just show me the kitchen and then I'll wheel in your chair and you can tell me where things are. We asked the doctor if you could come upstairs – I do hope you don't mind – and he said "Yes", if we helped you, so you might like to have your lunch up there with your sister. We can do two trays as easy as one and then you could stay up there for the party.'

'But Elizabeth, we cannot have a party here.'

'Yes, you can. We've asked the doctor and it's all fixed. It's got to be a quiet one but we're going to come and help celebrate your sister's birthday. You don't have to worry about a thing.'

'But even if the doctor did say it would not harm Gertrude, we have nothing here for a party, and you do not say how many there will be . . . It isn't suitable, my dear. We are quiet people and I am not strong and you must see that it wouldn't do. How many are coming – or how many were you going to ask if we could arrange it?'

'Just us two and three boys and maybe Sall's young sister, Veronica, and my brother, Hugh, but I s'pose he's too small . . . But you don't have to worry. We'll fix it all . . . Have you got any eggs?'

Then Sally came back. 'She's much better already. What are we going to cook or is it too early?'

And although they made a lot of mess and plenty of noise the girls did get two trays ready and before long Miss Mabel, in her wheeled chair, was laughing with them as they rummaged in the tiny larder.

'Toast,' Sally said. 'Whenever I'm ill I like toast. The crumbs get in the bed but I still like it. We must make Phelpy toast and cut the crusts off . . . I found an umbrella in the hall and took it up to her and she's going to bang on the floor if she wants anything.'

'I've been explaining about the party, Sall,' Elizabeth said as she put on an apron. 'We must keep it a surprise. We'll come at half-past three, very quietly, and you won't have to worry about anything, Miss Phelps. If you leave the door unlatched we can come straight in if you're resting.'

Miss Mabel gave up. She was used to being managed by her sister, but events now seemed to be out of her control, and even if these children were rather noisy they were certainly kind and cheerful, and perhaps the house would be the better for a little young life? But a birthday party for Gertrude arranged by strangers!

A little later she was helped upstairs and the chair hauled up after her without much difficulty, and the two sisters were left together while the omelettes and the toas were cooked.

'Now we've got to go,' a scarlet-faced Sally explained as she undid her borrowed apron. 'I do hope you've got everything but we've got a tremendous lot of most important things to do at home ... You've both got to remember that we're looking after you all the time today and some of us will come back and wash up presently ... Look after each other now and I'll tell Daddy you're much better already, shall I, Phelpy?'

'Yes indeed. I am very much better. I have not been spoiled like this for more years than I care to remember and these omelettes look quite delicious.'

'Cheerio for now then,' Elizabeth said. 'And don't you worry.'

'The things we've got to do!' Sally gasped as they pedalled furiously back to Nettleford. 'Do you think you could manage a birthday cake, Liza? We must have a cake for her.'

'With "Happy Returns to Phelpy" and how many candles? No, Sall. You ask your mother to help you with that. I'll make Scotch pancakes. I can do them. You just ladle the mixture on the hot-plate of our electric cooker and turn 'em over when they're done on one side. They're super ... Ring me up, Sall, as soon as you've had lunch ... I s'pose we all ought to bring her a present and I do wish we'd got more time. I wonder if Jimmy is about? See you later.'

Over the lunch table Sally told her story.

'Very well, Sall,' her mother said, 'I'll make a cake with soft icing and arrange the rest of the food except Elizabeth's contribution. I must go down in the shop soon and help Daddy but I think we can manage here between us. We'll send Phelpy some flowers and perhaps Veronica could see to that. If you stand on a chair could you cut some roses from the tree against the wall, darling?'

'Yes I could if I wear gloves. I want to give Phelpy something for her birthday by myself. I'll buy her a card.'

'What about Tony and me?' Paul said. 'If I'd had more time I might have caught her some fish.'

'You're always hoping,' Tony laughed. 'Lucky she hasn't got to rely on your fish else she'd starve to death! Jimmy's coming, by the way. He says he likes parties and that he can sing a song and said something about blacking his face. What can we take her besides Jimmy and his song?'

But in the end the birthday party was a great success. Soon after three, Sally took Paul and Tony round to Artillery Road. The door was open, so she made the boys take off their shoes and creep into the kitchen. Then she went up to the sisters, winked at Miss Mabel and said, 'I've brought Paul to wash up so now you can have a good rest until tea-time. We're arranging all that and we'll bring it up soon after four. How is your back, Phelpy?'

Phelpy indeed looked a different person. The lines of pain in her face were already softer and she moved much more easily in bed.

'I'm nothing but an old fraud, my dear, and I don't know what your father will think of me!'

'He says what we told you this morning. You're not to worry and we're all very, very sorry. He's managing quite well, he says, so long as he doesn't have to send any bills out, and Mummy says it's very good for him to see how much he misses you, and they both send their very best wishes.'

'Very kind,' Phelpy murmured. 'Very kind indeed. I can never remember being ill like this before but the pain has nearly gone already.'

Sally took the trays down one by one and then hissed at the boys:

'Don't you dare make a row. They think it's only Paul here. Wash these things up and then find all the cups and saucers and plates that you can and put them ready on the table. I'll go back for Liza and the cake. What about Jimmy?'

'He'll be here just before four,' Paul whispered. 'I'm so nervous, Sall, I'm sure I'll drop something. You ought not to leave us alone with all this crockery. Tell us what she looks like in bed?'

'You'll see her soon, idiot. Do make him behave himself, Tony.'

Elizabeth was at the *Wise Owl* when she got back.

'They're marvellous. Try one, Sall. I've had two but they're better with butter and jam . . . Just look at your mother's cake. Isn't it super?'

Margaret had also prepared sandwiches and by the time they were packed up Veronica appeared with an enormous bunch of roses.

'I've got a card too,' she said. 'A special one. I got it in the newspaper shop.'

Wilfred and Margaret came to the door to see them off and the former gave Sally an envelope for Phelpy. 'This is just to wish her well,' he said.

Jimmy, on his bicycle and carrying a small suitcase, caught them up at the end of Artillery Road.

'This is a rum go,' he said. 'Is it a wedding or a funeral?'

At twenty past four Sally and Elizabeth went into the sick room, announced that tea was nearly ready and opened up a gate-legged table. At twenty four minutes past Veronica was pushed ahead of the others, advanced to Phelpy's bed and thrust the roses at her without a word.

'Say it, you little idiot,' Paul muttered from the background.

Veronica gulped and looked up at the ceiling.

'All from the *Wise Owl* and our friends wish you a happy birthday and many happy returns,' she got out in a rush and then, led by Jimmy, the party broke into 'Happy Birthday to you'.

There was an awkward silence when the last strains died rather quaveringly away and then, to their horror, Phelpy, whom they had never known to be anything but abrupt, businesslike and to 'keep herself to herself' put her hands to her face and burst into tears.

'Thank you. Thank you,' she sobbed, but it was Sally who ran to her and put her arm round the thin shoulders and hugged her, feeling not very far from tears herself. Meanwhile Miss Mabel sat with her hands gripping the sides of her chair and with a bright spot of red on each cheek-bone.

'You're not to upset her,' she said. 'I told you it was wrong. I told you it would be too much for her.'

'But it isn't too much for me, Mabel,' Phelpy snuffled. 'It's wonderful. It's only too much kindness that makes me behave like a silly, doddering old woman ... These lovely flowers ... And a letter from Mr Richardson —'

'You should just see your birthday cake,' Paul broke in. 'You haven't seen a thing yet.'

'And you haven't heard a thing yet,' from Elizabeth. 'Jimmy is going to sing.'

'An' I've got a birthday card for you,' Veronica shrieked, feeling that she was rather out of the picture. 'Look at it *first*, please. You ought to do that – I'm the smallest.'

So while the boys went down for the trays of food Phelpy slit the grubby envelope which Veronica held out to her and then, when she had adjusted her spectacles, she sniffed again and fumbled for her handkerchief.

'Thank you, Veronica. It's a wonderful card. I'm sure you chose it yourself.'

Veronica simpered. 'Oh yes. I won't let them interfere with me.'

The card was without artistic merit. Forget-me-nots were much in evidence and the inscription read 'For my Best Friend'.

After tea, which was not after all a very quiet meal, the boys took down the trays and washed up and Veronica sat on the end of the invalid's bed and found, to her astonishment, that Phelpy was a most accomplished story-teller, while Elizabeth and Sally talked to Miss Mabel.

Then came the high-spot of the day, for Tony and Paul

came back without Jimmy who, they said, was getting ready.

Paul, who was the only one of the party who knew Jimmy really well, seemed to be very nervous. 'He's jolly good,' he said. 'We're going to do some turns together when we can find time to rehearse.'

There was then a weird, wailing sound from outside the door which opened suddenly to disclose an astonishing figure. They knew it to be Jimmy, of course, but there was nothing but a fringe of red hair under an old black hat to suggest it, for he was disguised as a nigger minstrel. His face was black except for his mouth which had a white oval round it like a clown's. He was wearing a one-piece overall which had been dyed black, and round his neck was a large white collar to which was fixed a floppy bow of some scarlet material.

He was received in a shocked silence which was broken by a steady clapping from Paul.

Jimmy then put to his mouth an unrecognizable metal instrument. Into this he hummed a haunting tune which brought a smile of understanding from Phelpy.

'Ah'm a' goin' to sing to you,' he then announced in a deep bass, and he sang a verse and the chorus of a song called *The Lily of Laguna*. Sally remembered hearing this once on the radio and Elizabeth, who had a quick ear, soon caught the refrain.

'She's ma lady love . . .'
and then 'She's the only queen Laguna knows,
'She's ma lily and ma rose.'

Jimmy was the leading treble in Mr Langton's choir. Music meant something to him and he sang this song so that they listened to him spellbound. Phelpy from her bed was gently beating out the time while her sister actually joined in the chorus.

'Again,' Veronica pleaded. 'I like it, Jimmy.'

'I do know some others,' he said in his ordinary voice. 'I know *Swanee River*. My dad taught them to me.'

'Teach us *Laguna*,' Tony said. 'I've never heard it before.'

'It's old-fashioned but it's all right,' Jimmy grinned, and then he started again. As they caught the words as well as the melody he produced his instrument and accompanied them, but in the middle of the last chorus Miss Mabel looked up and, to her horror, noticed a woman she had never seen before standing smiling at them in the doorway behind Jimmy. And when she too began to sing, Veronica slid off the end of the bed and with a cry of 'Mummy', dodged past the nigger mistrel and almost knocked her over with her welcome.

'Forgive me for coming up, but the front door was unlatched and there was too much noise for you to hear the bell. I've come to send the children home and see if Miss Phelps has survived the ordeal. What a lovely, sunny room this is!'

She greeted Phelpy, shook hands with Miss Mabel and took the chair which Paul brought over.

'Off you go now,' she said to them all. 'I'm going to stay a little while and see what I can do. Leave everything tidy downstairs.' Then she added, 'I am sorry to have interrupted you, Jimmy. I thought you were wonderful. I love that tune too.'

'Now you know what was in my bag,' Jimmy said

to the girls when they were outside. 'Was it all right? Honest?'

'Honest it was,' Sally said. 'I dare you to walk home in that outfit.'

'I will if I can come into the *Wise Owl* and change. I'll get into a row from Dad if he sees me. Or maybe I could change in the vicarage?'

'Not likely,' Liza said hurriedly. 'I wouldn't mind, but the parents might. I dare you to walk up to your Dad's shop like that.'

'Leave him alone,' Paul said. 'Mr Brand teaches him those songs and made him that suit. It might be bad for business if he walked about Nettleford like that.'

'All right, Jimmy. We'll let you off. I'll ask Dad one day if you could parade about like that in the town advertising the *Wise Owl* . . . Do you think Phelpy enjoyed it?'

'Yes, I do,' Veronica said. 'She cried a bit but she liked it . . . So do I . . .'

And, after Jimmy had removed his disguise, they all went home together, pushing their bicycles and humming *Lily of Laguna*.

7

BEULAH

LUCKILY for the Richardsons, Phelpy was only in bed for three days after her birthday and was then persuaded by them and the doctor to go away for a week with her sister.

This holiday was Wilfred's idea because he was feeling rather guilty about her, but they all helped to get the two sisters away and by the time they were back the Richardsons were ready for their holiday at Tenby. Tony was coming with them.

Way back in January Wilfred had arranged with a Mrs Robins to let them three bedrooms and a sitting-room and cook for them so that Margaret had no housework. The house was called *Beulah* and the road, South Bay Drive, which sounded magnificent.

It wasn't really magnificent, but they all loved Tenby as soon as they stepped on to the platform and Wilfred fussed round the guard's van in search of their luggage.

'I can't see the sea,' Veronica complained. 'I want it.'

'Sniff,' Sally said. 'You can smell it.'

The houses in South Bay Drive were all alike and rather ugly, but Mrs Robins welcomed them warmly in a Welsh sing-song as they crowded into the hall while Wilfred was paying off the taxi-driver.

It was after six and after tea in their sitting-room on the first floor that Margaret and Wilfred sent the children out to explore.

Veronica was white with excitement when at last they found the thrilling road that led down to the sea. Below them in the evening sunshine they saw the harbour, gay with little boats at rest on the unruffled blue water. Then they explored the harbour wall and watched some men and boys fishing. ('This is where I'll be every day,' Paul whispered to Tony.) Next they ran down to the sands and paddled as the tide slipped out, and then climbed a hill to see the coastguard's look-out, and found on the other side a bigger bay with a sweep of sand at least two miles long. A steady breeze from the sea ruffled their hair and brought with it the unforgettable smell of seaweed and damp sand and salt water.

'What I want to know,' Veronica said, 'is whether we can go anywhere we like on all that sand whenever we like.'

They reassured her and went back to supper at *Beulah* where their luggage was now unpacked and where the rows of books and maps on the mantelpiece reminded them of home.

At first the days seemed endless and each was very like the next. Sometimes they played cricket with other families on the sands and always they bathed before lunch. At half-past twelve they strolled back to *Beulah* across the loose, hot sand up the slope where the deck-chairs were stacked and into South Bay Drive. Every day Mrs Robins gave them sandwiches, cakes and flasks of tea to take back to the beach. It was then that Margaret and Wilfred dozed in the sun while Veronica played her own secret games in her own way. They loved too the lazy hours between tea and supper, when they were all pleasantly tired and soaked in the sun, and, and often walked barefoot along the edge of the tide to the far end of the bay. Most evenings after supper, Wilfred read aloud to them and once they all – including Veronica – went to a concert party.

And so day followed leisurely day and nothing very much happened until the last day but one when the weather changed and they were driven indoors by the fury of a gale. Great white-capped waves swept up the deserted beaches. The horizon vanished in a flurry of rain and the windows of *Beulah* rattled as the children squabbled with boredom and Veronica announced that she wanted to go home.

All through the night the storm raged, but when they came down to breakfast on the last day of a wonderful holiday, the rain had stopped and the sky showed some patches of blue between the scudding clouds.

'Before one of you asks what you're going to do today because you can't go on the beach, I'll tell you,' Wilfred said as he sat down to breakfast. 'Your mother isn't coming down yet. She's got a headache and wants to rest, so Veronica is going to stay with me and look after her. You boys and Sally might take the bus to the village called Lydstep where there are some caves, and come back over the cliffs by the big headland we see every day . . . Here's the map which shows you the field paths, and you could come home the last two miles along the beach, if it's not too rough, and here's some money to buy yourselves some lunch.'

Sally ran up to see her mother before they left and was relieved to find her quite cheerful and looking forward to a morning in bed.

'Have a good day and look after each other,' she smiled. 'We shall want to hear all about your expedition when you get back.'

The bus was late, and the conductor explained that they'd been held up by a fallen tree across the road. They sat on the front seats on the top deck, where they could see the grey and forbidding sea and the rugged coastline of cliffs, and all the time the wind roared and boomed round the bus so that Sally was very pleased to get out in the village street of Lydstep.

Wilfred had told them to walk back a little way until they came to a track leading down to a bay where caves were actually marked on the map. He had shown them, too, the thin, dotted line along the top of the cliffs to the jagged point known as Proud Giltar which marked the path home to Tenby. It was not more than five miles to walk, and would have been easy on a fine day if he had been with them. But Wilfred, perhaps because he was anxious about Margaret, had forgotten to warn them that on such a day the cliff path would almost certainly be deserted. Neither had he realized what the force of the gale would be two hundred feet up on the unprotected limestone headland.

They found the track which led them down to the beach of a little bay where great white-capped waves pounded the shingle with a thunderous roar. Away to their left towered Proud Giltar, but if there were any caves at beach level they were hidden today in a cloud of spray.

Sally clung to her brother and shouted,

'I hate this place. Let's go back to the top of the cliff. This is a silly day for a walk.'

Paul nodded and they turned back the way they had come, and when the path forked they took the right-hand turn and struggled up through bracken and heather.

When they reached the top of the first hill they saw, unexpectedly, below them a whitewashed cottage in a hollow. Just before they reached it a woman came out to the gate.

'Where have you come from?' she said as they came up.

'Up from the bay,' Sally replied. 'Why?'

'Any of you see my boy, Johnnie? He's got a dog with him.'

'We haven't seen anybody,' Paul explained. 'What shall we say if we meet him? We're going to Tenby.'

'Send him back here, if you please, and take care as you go over the top. It's not the day for walking over Giltar. Keep away from the edge and mind the potholes,' and she went in and slammed the door.

'Funny place to live,' Tony shouted as they went on. 'Wonder what she meant by potholes?'

Sally did not answer. She was beginning to wish that they had gone back to the road and returned home by bus.

For ten minutes they fought their way forward with tears streaming from their eyes and the spray salt on their lips. Then, at the top of a rise, Paul looked up and then stopped in surprise.

'Look!' he yelled. 'There's the boy.'

Below them in a hollow was the opening of a great chasm or pit about ten yards wide running at right angles to the edge of the cliff, and on the lip of this awful pothole they saw the straddled body of a small boy leaning, face down, over the edge as if he was trying to reach something they could not see. Sally felt a scream rising in her throat as Tony yelled something over his shoulder as he raced ahead down the hill. Paul grabbed her hand and they tore after their cousin, with the wind almost lending them wings.

They saw the strange boy run towards Tony and make a gesture with one hand. And as he moved he slipped and suddenly he was no longer on the edge of the abyss but clutching at the slippery grass and then disappearing from their terrified gaze.

They saw Tony fling himself forward and almost before they realized that they had moved they too were on their knees beside him. A few feet below them was a grassy ledge about a yard across at its greatest width and here, clinging to a stunted thorn tree with one arm, was a white-faced boy of about ten. In his other arm he was clutching a little brown dog.

Below the ledge was an awful, narrowing funnel with rough sides of whitened rock sliding down into a horrible nothingness. Sally noticed that the boy's mouth was open as if he were trying to speak and that the sweat was running down his face.

'You're all right,' Tony was shouting. 'Don't move and we'll get you up . . . *And don't look down!*' and then she had to turn over on her face as she was swept by a wave of sickness. Paul's voice – hoarse and so unlike his usual way of speaking – came to her from a long way off.

'What shall we do, Tony? Can we pull him up?'

'We could reach him with the belts off our raincoats, but we'll have to get help. Run back to the cottage, Paul. You're the best runner. Sall will stay with me, but leave your raincoat . . .'

She turned over again and grass and sky and the cruel, grey sea swept round her in a dizzy circle.

'O.K. I'll be back with someone,' Paul shouted as he flung down his coat and battled back the way they had come.

Tony, with a face as white as the other boy's, glanced quickly at Sally.

'Keep talking to him, Sall. *He mustn't look down.*'

'I *can't*, Tony. I'm sick. I can't look over.'

'You must. If I can you can. Keep talking to him and I'll fix these belts together.'

Sally gulped, took a deep breath and looked over the edge.

'You're Johnnie, aren't you?' she yelled.

The boy nodded and then looked down at the dog. He was half on his knees facing them, with one foot over the edge, and as he fell or was blown over by the wind he must have clutched at the thorn tree instinctively and so saved his life. But it was a very little tree and Sally felt sick again as she wondered whether it would hold.

'Yes,' he said. 'Can you get me up? Foxy fell over in the wind and I couldn't leave him, could I? Could you get him up first?'

Sally could never recall all the things that happened after that. She knew that her courage returned as she realized that if they could keep Johnnie from thinking about himself until someone came with a rope, they could surely save him. Vaguely she remembered Tony buckling together the three belts from their raincoats, and then –

'My arms feel funny,' the boy whimpered. 'My knees are moving too. I want to get out of here.'

Then Tony lowered the rope made of the three belts.

'If you could stand up, Johnnie, and hold on the end of this maybe we could pull you up.'

He looked bewildered and his lip quivered as he realized that he would have to let go either of the tree or the dog to grasp his life-line. The two rescuers realized this at the same moment.

'I can't,' Johnnie sobbed. 'Foxy has hurt his foot and if I put him down he'll slip. He's scared, you see . . . I think this tree moved then.'

Sally fought back her own tears.

'Foxy,' she called, and the dog pricked up his ears. 'Foxy boy. We've got to pull you up first.'

'How can you?' Johnnie gasped. 'Please be quick and help me.'

Then Tony said, 'Sall. If I slid down to the ledge and passed the dog up to you, could you reach him by leaning over and holding on to the end of these belts as well? We've got to get the dog away from him.'

Sally had a fearful vision of Tony slipping and pulling her over with him.

'I can't, Tony. I can't. I couldn't do it.'

'You'll have to let Foxy go for a second, Johnnie,' Tony went on. 'Put him on the grass in front of you. He won't fall. I'll drop the belts and you can thread one end under his collar still holding on to the tree with your arm. Go on, Johnnie. *You've got to do it.* You've got to do what I say.'

Strangely enough, he did. The dog lay panting and whining on the ledge while he pushed the belt under his collar and then threaded the free end through the buckle and pulled it tight like a slip-knot.

'Now I'm going to lean over as far as I can,' Tony went on, 'and you've got to throw me the end of the belts and then we'll pull Foxy up . . . Sally. Stop snivelling. Get

back a bit and hold on to my ankles for all you're worth
. . . Don't argue . . . Ready? Right, Johnnie . . .'

And next moment, with a half-strangled yelp, a lovely
Welsh Corgi was up on the turf beside her and licking her
face as she undid the belts from his collar. Tony wriggled
back beside her and grabbed the belts again.

'Now hang on to this with your free hand, Johnnie, and
you'll be O.K. We're on the other end.'

They talked to him again after this. He was kneeling
upright still clasping the tree, but although he answered
them sometimes they could see that his strength and will-
power were failing and although it seemed like hours of
waiting, actually only twenty minutes had passed before
a shout from the top of the hill told them that their ordeal
was nearly over. A man in a cap and with a coil of rope
over his shoulder was racing down the slope towards
them.

'Go and meet him, Sall. Tell him it's all right . . . O.K.
Johnnie. Hold on. Here comes a man and a rope.'

The man was Johnnie's father but Sally only managed
to say a few words before, 'God bless you kids,' he gasped,
as he flung himself down beside Tony. 'Here's your Dad,
Johnnie boy. You do what I say now and nothing else.
Give me the end of those belts, lad.'

Tony passed them over, moved back and rolled over.
Blood was trickling from a bitten lip and his hair was
dank on his forehead. Sally could find no words, but with
an odd little gesture she put out her hand and touched his
on the grass beside her. He smiled and sat up.

'Shucks, as Paul would say. What do we do now?'

But now there was somebody else to take the responsibility. The man made Johnnie leave go of the tree, grasp the belts with both hands and then stand up with his face to the rocks.

Then he dropped a noose of the rope over the boy's outstretched arms and told him to let go of the belts and tighten the slip-knot round his chest. A minute later he was safe in his father's arms and the dog was dancing round them all.

Once again the wind brought them a welcome hail and they looked up to see Paul and the boy's mother waving from the crest of the hill. Sally shouted and waved back and ran up to meet them.

'Johnnie is safe,' she yelled. 'We've got him up,' and then to her brother she said something which he never forgot. 'Jolly well run, Paul. Nobody could have been quicker.'

Mr and Mrs Davies – for that was the name of Johnnie's parents – insisted that the children went back with them to the cottage and they were too tired to argue or to face again the ordeal of the cliff walk. Johnnie was carried home on his father's back and packed off to bed without protest as soon as they got in. There was not much room for them all in the living-room but it was wonderful to sit down in the warm away from the wind.

Mr Davies made tea while his wife was upstairs with Johnnie and they all felt better for it, but when he started once again to thank them for all they had done they fidgeted with embarrassment and Paul got up to go.

'Our parents will be worried about us, Mr Davies. We must get back to the road and catch the bus.'

'That you will not do. No buses for you. Back in the

hired car from Lydstep and David Davies pays. Proud I shall be. I will come with you to the telephone and wait until the car comes.'

But it was Mrs Davies who took the children to a shed and showed them a litter of sturdy Corgi pups.

'They are ready to leave their mother. Perhaps you would like one each? Take them, my dears, to remind you of Johnnie Davies.'

'We can't,' Sally said. 'I've got a puppy waiting for me at home but why don't you take one, Tony? You're going home next week and you were the one who really saved Johnnie . . . I haven't told you yet, Paul, how marvellous he was.'

'Mother wouldn't let me keep one in the flat,' Tony said as he picked up a squirming, brown puppy who nibbled at his fingers.

'Risk it!' Sally said. 'We'll explain how it happened. Take him now and call him Proud Giltar.'

8

SALLY TAKES CHARGE

JUST as the last few days at Tenby had slipped by too quickly, so did the summer and the waning school holidays seem to stretch their wings for flight as soon as the Richardsons came back to Nettleford.

They arrived on the Saturday evening after the *Wise Owl* had closed, but Phelpy had stayed to welcome them and had even got tea ready. This was the first of many compensations for coming home and perhaps the next was the joy of having their own things round them again and sleeping in their own beds.

'I love holidays,' Sally remarked as she went over to the window and looked down Nettleford's familiar High Street, 'but home is always better than anywhere else.'

Another compensation was Jimmy, who winked at them shamelessly as he processed round the church in the choir on Sunday morning. He came to tea later, was introduced to the puppy and told the story of Johnnie Davies. In turn he told them that Elizabeth and her family were away until Wednesday, and this annoyed Sally because she had sent her friend two postcards and one letter and had nothing in reply.

'Have you been over to Northend?' Paul said. 'I wonder how they're getting on?'

'No time. I've been jolly busy. Been helping Dad a bit but I reckoned we could go over there one day this week . . . You learned to swim yet, young Vee?'

'Nearly I can. I do it better when there's not too much water underneath me.'

'Have you been doing any more singing, Jimmy?' Margaret asked as she passed him a slice of cake. 'I heard you this morning in church, of course, but I meant any public or special performances?'

Jimmy winked. 'I got some ideas about that . . . I'm saving up for a banjo and that's one thing. Another is that I reckon we ought to put on a show by ourselves at Christmas.'

'A show?' Paul asked. 'What d'you mean, Jimmy?'

'Sort of concert party or a play. I got a lot of ideas . . . I say!' he put down a half-consumed corner of cake. 'I got another idea. You know about the big fête there's going to be in the vicarage field? What the vicar calls the Furnace Fête?'

They nodded, remembering that this particular event had been arranged some months ago in order to raise enough money to put a new heating system in the church.

'That's right, Jimmy,' Margaret said. 'It's in a fortnight's time. I'm on the Household Stall. What's your idea?'

'It's not really for grown-ups,' he replied, 'but it's a super scheme. I was wondering whether we could put on a show of our own inside the big fête – just us, I mean, and Elizabeth, o' course, when she comes back. What d'you think, Sall?'

'Marvellous, Jimmy. We'll start making plans today and settle everything when Liza comes back on Wednesday. She doesn't deserve it, but we'll have to have her in. It will be our last Saturday before school, won't it? Why are you looking so miserable, Tony?'

'I'll be home by then, I s'pose. Mother said they'd be back next week and I'm expecting a letter in the morning . . . I won't know what to do in London by myself.'

Nobody seemed to be able to answer this and indeed all round the tea table were thinking that in different ways Tony would certainly be missed.

'Oh, well, Tony,' his aunt said at last, 'I shouldn't worry about that yet. You can stay here as long as you like, you know. Seems silly to remember that we were afraid that you wouldn't enjoy yourself with us, doesn't it? Wait till we get some news of your mother and father and then perhaps we'll ring up and see what they say . . . Now you'd better all go out and take young Giltar with you. He's safer out of doors.'

But the blow fell next morning when Sally came up from the shop with the post and gave her cousin a brightly coloured postcard of an Italian scene.

'I've got to go Wednesday,' he said gloomily. 'They'll be back then and the housekeeper will be opening up the flat. Mother says she expects me to be there . . . I'd like to stay, if you'll have me, but I think I ought to go.'

'I think you should too, my boy,' Wilfred said. 'We've enjoyed having you and you'll always be welcome. Come at Christmas and help in the shop.'

'Maybe I could come down for the weekend of the fête?' Tony suggested. 'I must come and see your show.'

Jimmy had told them that the fête was being organized by a Major Knight, a rather terrifying old gentleman who lived on the outskirts of the town and was to be seen on Sundays in the churchwardens' pew. As the vicar would not be back until Wednesday they had already decided to see the major as soon as they could and offer their services to him.

'You'd better come with us, Tony, even if you are going home on Wednesday,' Sally said after breakfast. 'I think we can manage him and then we'll make our plans today and have everything ready for Liza. I think we shall have to get some more people to help us. Maybe Charles would.'

'Of course I'll come . . . As I'm going so soon do you think we could go out for the day tomorrow and call in at Northend and see them? I'd like to go there again.'

They agreed that this was a good idea and went out to collect Jimmy, after constructing a small pen for young Giltar in the back garden. Mr Quirk hailed them from his doorstep as they went down the street.

'Five beauties yesterday, Sally. I've not forgotten my promise. Come in this evening and see them . . . Nice to have you all back again.'

The major was standing on the edge of a very yellow drive in front of his house, glaring at two daisies which had dared to show their faces on his lawn. He was small and neat with an eye-glass and a little moustache, but Sally knew very well that although he looked fierce he was kind enough if you weren't afraid of him. She knew that he collected butterflies and often came into the *Wise Owl* to see if there were any new books on natural history.

'Good morning, Major,' she said. 'Please may we come and speak to you about your fête? We want to help.'

''Morning, Sally,' he barked. 'Look at those daisies. Came up in the night when I was asleep. Went over every inch of the lawn yesterday . . . What are you doing with all those boys? One of 'em's your brother isn't he? Always forget his name . . . And that's young Brand from the choir! You're a young devil, Brand. I was watching you yesterday in the sermon. Who's the other boy and what's all this about the fête? Want all the help we can get, of course . . . Don't stand there gaping. Come in and close the gate.'

He led the way to the garden at the back of the house and sat them in a row on a hard seat placed with geometrical precision under a glass-roofed veranda.

'Lemonade?' he barked. 'Of course you will.' He opened the french windows. 'Four lemonades please, Mrs Huggins,' and his housekeeper appeared with a tray so quickly that Jimmy, who was a trifle nervous, imagined that she must have known they were coming!

Sally continued to act as spokesman and was not put off by the major's glare as he stood in front of them with his hands behind his back.

'. . . Of course we're not quite sure *exactly* what we can do yet, and how many of us there will be, but if you could rope off a corner of the field and p'raps give us a small tent we'll have a stall and sell things which we'll collect ourselves, and maybe we'll have a fortune-teller, and Jimmy will do his act and Elizabeth and me could sell cakes and Veronica flower posies . . .'

She stopped to take a new breath and Paul took up the tale.

'We've hardly started on our ideas yet but we shall sell tickets in advance and I bet we make a lot of money for you. Just you leave it to us, sir, and we'll show you how to make a fête go . . .'

157

The major's eye-glass dropped from his eye and tinkled against a button of his yellow waistcoat.

'I believe you would, by Jove. I shall have to consult my committee, of course, and have a word with the vicar on his return, but you can take it that your offer is accepted. Excellent idea. A show by the children of the parish . . . Have another glass of lemonade . . . Mrs Huggins!'

They spent the afternoon under the willow tree by the river writing down a number of startling ideas in a note-book. Tony had not much to say and once, when Paul asked him if he was dumb, Sally kicked him gently just to remind him that their cousin was not feeling very cheerful at the thought of Wednesday.

When they got home Wilfred told them that he was not much enjoying his first day back at work and that he had telephoned Northend and told the Wilkins that they would probably see the children tomorrow.

Tomorrow came quickly enough and they were all too excited at breakfast to notice that Margaret was quieter than usual. Only when she was cutting their sandwiches did Sally notice that she was sitting down to do so.

'Are you all right, Mummy? Are you tired?'

'A little darling, but I haven't got much to do today. Don't look so worried. Give Tony a good day for his last. Are you sorry he's going?'

Sally flushed.

'Yes. I think I am but it will be fun for us just to be together again. Just the five of us I mean. Our family is fun isn't it, Mummy?'

And later that day – the longest day in her short life – Sally remembered what she had said standing there by the kitchen table watching the sunlight on her mother's head, and the way in which she had looked up at her and smiled and said, 'Always remember that, Sall.'

At breakfast Veronica had made a direct appeal to Tony to be allowed to come with them.

'I can walk farther than you think . . . We could go some of the way by bus and I WANT TO GO WITH TONY today.'

And so Veronica was included in the party and the expedition took a long time in consequence. Jimmy came with them, of course, and although they had a map they lost their way between the main road where the bus put them down and the hill with the clump of pine trees.

They had their lunch at a spring, and then, in the drowsy afternoon, wandered slowly down the valley towards Northend.

Sally was in front when they came out of the shadows and looked across the field where they had camped to the farmhouse below. The roofs of the barns glowed in the sunshine, and in the rickyard the big golden ricks stood serene and proud, and at the front gate they saw a familiar figure.

'It's Aunt Mary!' she said. 'Tell her we're here,' and they yelled and waved until Mrs Wilkins raised an arm in answer and crossed the lane to the field gate.

'She's coming to meet us,' Paul said. 'I'll race anyone down.'

Although he got there first it was not really a race because Sally ran with Vee and Tony stayed with them both. Paul and Jimmy were too breathless to say much, but when Sally came up to greet Mrs Wilkins she saw something in her face that set her heart thumping.

Aunt Mary stooped and swept Veronica off her feet into her arms as Sally said, 'Were you waiting for us, Aunt Mary? Is anything wrong?'

Veronica had always been Mrs Wilkins's favourite, perhaps because she had been the youngest and the easiest to spoil, and because she was a girl. Paul was rough and noisy and Sally, just beginning to grow up, had often puzzled her. But now as she looked at the eldest Richardson over Veronica's curls she caught her breath as she noticed the challenging tilt of the child's head and the suggestion of puzzled fear in the grey eyes so like her mother's.

She made up her mind. It would be no use beating about the bush with these Richardson children. She stepped forward and put a hand on Sally's shoulder.

'You've got to be brave,' she said. 'I've bad news for you, but thank God you've come back this way for I've been wondering for two hours how to find you with John away at market —'

'*What is it, Aunt Mary?* Is is something to do with mummy? Please, *please* tell us.'

Veronica slid to the ground and grabbed her sister's hand and Mrs Wilkins tried again.

'Your father telephoned, Sally. Your mother is ill and has been taken to hospital. He has gone with her and you are all to stay here until he telephones again.'

The long silence that followed was broken by a frightened wail from Veronica. Jimmy stuffed his hands in his pockets and looked away so that he could not see the fear in the faces of his friends. Paul, with a lump in his throat, opened his mouth for a question that would not come and Tony, too, was speechless.

Sally felt the blood draining from her face and for a moment swayed as if she would fall. Then –

'How ill is she? She's not dead, Aunt Mary? Don't you dare to tell us a lie. How ill is she?'

'I don't know, child. By what your father said I think she has to have an operation . . . You mustn't feel like that, love. People are having operations every day. Doctors are wonderful. She will be all right and you'll have her home soon enough . . . Come now to the house for your father may ring any time,' and she took Veronica by the hand and led the way back to the gate

'Oh gosh!' Jimmy said. 'I feel awful. Would you like me to go?'

'But *Mother*?' Paul whispered. 'But we've only just left her. She cut our sandwiches. She was all right —'

'She wasn't all right,' Sally said in a shaky voice. 'She was ill this morning. I saw she was different but she said she was just tired. Don't you remember she was ill at Tenby too – the day we went to Giltar – and I saw she was ill this morning and I went out and left her and now she's in hospital and I'll never, *never* forgive myself. What shall we *do*, Paul? We can't stay here with her all those miles away in a strange place.'

'I shouldn't think you could,' Tony said unexpectedly, 'but it might not be a bad idea to leave Vee here – and don't scare her too much, Sally.'

Sally looked at her cousin with respect and then, just as they were crossing the lane, they heard the sound of the telephone bell ringing in the hall of the house.

'I'll answer it,' she shouted. 'Yes, I will, Aunt Mary. It's Daddy and I've got to speak to him,' and she rushed past Mrs Wilkins and Veronica and grabbed the receiver.

'Hullo! . . . Oh, Daddy. It's me. Sally. We've only just got here. Is Mummy all right?'

The dear, familiar voice came faintly over the wire.

'Steady, Sally. Steady . . . Yes, darling. Your mother is not in pain now and they will operate this evening . . . I shall stay here in the hospital until that is over and you had all better stop at the farm —'

'No, Daddy, *please*! We don't want to do that. Vee will stay with Aunt Mary and we shall come home right away. We *must* be at home. It's the place to be and we shall sit in the shop until you telephone again, but we must come home —'

'Steady, Sall! You must be brave and sensible. You are the eldest and I trust you. The last thing your mother said to me was, "Sally will look after you until I come back" ' – and here her father's voice broke a little and Sally herself changed a sob into a choky laugh.

'I will, Daddy. I will. You can trust me . . . Now speak to Aunt Mary and tell her we're coming home at once,' and she passed over the receiver and turned to the boys.

'She's safe in hospital and she's going to have an operation tonight. Vee will stay here and we'll go home.'

She went down on her knees and put her arms round her sister.

'Listen, poppet. Daddy has taken Mummy to hospital for a few days until she's better. He wants you to stay with Aunt Mary and look after her. *Please* don't make a face.'

Veronica gulped and complained that she was always

being left out of things and then Mrs Wilkins replaced the telephone and said, 'I want you to stay and look after me and Uncle John and the ducks, Veronica. Just for a few days until your mother is back and then you'll have to look after her . . . You others had better go back if you've made up your minds, but remember that you're welcome at any time. I don't know how you'll manage but you've plenty of friends in the town I've no doubt . . . Sally, my love. You'd better take some eggs with you. It's wonderful what you can do with eggs . . . I'm sorry your uncle is out with the car but it won't take you so long to walk up to the bus . . .'

Ten minutes later they were on their way, leaving Veronica and Aunt Mary waving again and again at the gate. Up the hill they went and turned at the top as they always did to look at the farmhouse in the valley, and then on through the avenue of beeches which reminded Sally and Paul so much of their mother.

'Let me know if I can do anything,' Jimmy said awkwardly when they left him in the High Street. 'You know what I mean . . . I reckon I'll come across presently – just in case.'

They knew what he meant and there was no need to say anything as they ran the last twenty yards to the *Wise Owl* and pushed through the door together.

Phelpy was talking to Major Knight and they both stopped when Sally said, 'We spoke to Daddy on the phone. Is there any more news?'

'No more news except that Mrs Richardson is fairly comfortable and that the operation is at six o'clock,' Phelpy said while the major cleared his throat noisily, put down a ten-shilling note on the counter and, glaring fiercely at Paul, said, 'Very sorry indeed to hear the news. Don't you worry. Appendicitis is nothing these days. Buy your mother some books with this. Send her my best wishes . . . 'Afternoon, Miss Phelps . . . 'Bye, Sally.'

As soon as he had gone Paul said, 'We have to come home, Phelpy. It was Sall's idea. We can help you and look after Dad a bit when he comes back. He told Sall that she's in charge upstairs. Vee's staying at Northend . . . We'd better go up and get tea.'

Phelpy's eyes were moist as she looked at them affection-ately. 'Don't you fret, my dears. She'll be all right and as soon as I can close the shop I'll be upstairs to help you.'

'You've got to go and look after Miss Mabel,' Sally smiled. 'We know your secret now, Phelpy.'

They hated it upstairs. The kitchen table was covered with cooking things just as they had been left so suddenly. In their parents' bedroom drawers and cupboards were open and Margaret's bed was unmade and an eiderdown and hot water-bottle on the floor. Everywhere were signs of haste and disorder.

'Let's *do* something,' Paul said gruffly. 'Let's try and tidy up a bit and get some tea. No use glooming about the place like this.'

They went back to the kitchen and Tony lit the gas under the kettle.

'I shan't go home tomorrow,' he said. 'I've made up my mind. I can be of more help here – if you want me, of course.'

Sally remembered what she had said about the family being together and now the family was broken up and

Tony was offering to stay. She wasn't sure just then whether she wanted him or not, but she knew that it was kind of him to offer. It would be easier tonight to give the right answer, when they knew more. People kept saying that everything was going to be all right and none of the family had ever had an operation before, except Paul who had had his tonsils out, but this was different. Her mother must be very ill to have been rushed off like that in just a few hours. She had often heard people say that it was difficult to get into hospitals so this must be very urgent. Then she thought of her father and of how worried he must be. And how lonely, too, if they wouldn't let him sit with her.

'You boys get the tea,' she said suddenly, 'I'm going to see Phelpy for a sec.'

Downstairs she had to wait until Phelpy had finished with a woman who was saying, 'I know it sounds rather silly but I always think the best love stories have orange covers,' but before the door had closed behind this unusual customer she said, 'Phelpy. Do *please* help me. I want to ask you something awful . . . Please, Phelpy, will you give me – of course it's only lending until Daddy comes back – but I want five shillings out of the till. I haven't any money except eightpence and I must have at least five shillings *at once*.'

'Of course, my dear. I'll lend it to you myself. Do you want to buy something for your tea?'

'No. I'll tell you why I want it. I'm going to the hospital. I think Daddy ought to have somebody with him while he's waiting, and I'm the one to go. The others will manage I'm sure.'

Phelpy looked steadily at her for a long minute and then went into her little glass box for her handbag.

'Very well, Sally. I don't know whether I should tell you not to go but I believe you are right and that your father would like you with him. Here is a ten-shilling note. You can give it me back tomorrow.'

'Thank you, Phelpy. You're wonderful,' and she ran upstairs and told the boys her plan.

'As soon as Phelpy has gone, one of you will have to sit in the shop until we telephone. You can't hear it from up here. You'll manage, won't you? Put some tea in a Thermos and we'll make some sandwiches. I don't suppose Daddy will have had anything to eat.'

But when at last she was in the bus she felt lonely and afraid. It seemed ridiculous that none of her fellow passengers knew what was happening to the Richardson family and she hated the way in which they chattered and laughed. She suddenly realized that she wasn't sure where the hospital was and wondered even whether they would let her in. Perhaps they closed at five and it was nearly half-past already? And perhaps when she got there her father would have left? She clutched her basket and stared ahead at the familiar road along which she went every day to school. Her mouth was dry and she felt a little sick with fear and excitement when she asked a woman at the bus stop the way to the hospital. It somehow seemed wrong that the evening should be so beautiful as she walked, ten minutes later, feeling very small and alone, along the drive and then up the steps of the big building. She pushed open the swing-doors and the unmistakable hospital smell made her catch her breath.

Everything was very clean and bright. A man in uniform in a glass-fronted office looked at her over his spectacles and said:

'What do you want, miss? It's past visiting hours.'

Sally took a deep breath and tried to keep her voice from shaking.

'My mother is having her operation at six o'clock. My father is waiting here by himself and I want to see him. I've brought him some tea.'

'What name, miss?'

She told him. He consulted a list and nodded. Over his shoulder she saw the hands of a clock pointing to ten minutes past six.

'*Please* let me see him. I can't do any harm, can I?'

The porter pushed his spectacles up his forehead.

'For all I know it's against the rules,' he said, 'but you come along o' me, young miss, and if the telephone rings, it rings.'

He came out into the hall and unexpectedly took her hand, and Sally was so surprised that she squeezed his rough fingers. Together they walked down the long hall and she was reminded somehow of a scene in some film she had once seen. A nurse passed them briskly with a curious glance and then her new friend opened a door marked 'Waiting Room'.

'Visitor for Mr Richardson,' he announced and pushed Sally gently into the room. An old man, with shaking hands and a young woman were sitting at a table turning over magazines, but by the window was her father. His shoulders seemed a little more bowed than usual and his hair more untidy. The spotted, blue bow-tie was askew, but his eyes lit up as Sally dropped her basket, rushed forward and flung her arms round him.

'I had to come, Daddy. I couldn't bear you being alone, an' I've brought your tea!'

He bent and kissed the top of her shining head and even if she did cry a little the tears were not altogether unhappy. She rubbed her cheek against his rough, tweedy sleeve and sniffed the smell of cloth and tobacco and shaving soap which she loved so much.

'Thank you, darling,' he said. 'How like you to come,' and then he put a hand on her shoulder and turned to their two companions who were gazing at them in astonishment. 'My elder daughter,' he said proudly. 'We shall be outside in the sunshine. Perhaps if I am wanted you would be kind enough to call me . . . Come, Sally.'

They passed the porter in his box.

'This is my father,' Sally announced unnecessarily. 'We are going outside. Please will you call us when — when it's time?'

'It's against the rules I expect,' the man replied, 'but we'll let you know.'

They found a seat but neither of them could eat. Sally had forgotten to bring cups so they shared the tea from the top of the flask and both burned their fingers. It would not be fair to tell you everything that they said to each other during that time of waiting, but Sally did tell him that, on the bus, she had remembered so many of the horrid, unkind things she had said to her mother and of how she had often been rude and hurt her.

'I s'pose I'm being punished now, Daddy. I s'pose I

deserve it. I s'pose God's showing me. I'd promise Him *anything* if only Mummy is all right.'

'I don't think we can make bargains like that, Sall. I mean it doesn't just seem right to ask for things we want when things go wrong, does it? But I know how you feel. I have been remembering things like that, too.'

Twice they went back to the porter, who shook his head.

'We'll go back in five minutes,' Wilfred said as he looked at his watch as they walked up and down the drive, but before that time was up Sally looked back over her shoulder and saw a nurse waving to them from the steps.

'Stay here, Sally,' Wilfred said sharply, but she took no notice as the nurse came smiling to meet them.

'Your wife has had her operation, Mr Richardson. The surgeon is satisfied and she is as well as can be expected. You may come and see her for a few minutes tomorrow and telephone in the morning.'

She smiled and nodded and went back up the steps. She had red hair and was very pretty.

Somewhere near a thrush burst into unexpected song and when Sally clutched her father's arm and looked up and saw the expression on his face she said, 'It's the loveliest evening I remember . . . We must telephone the others.'

And this is exactly what her mother would have said.

9

FURNACE FÊTE

THE next ten days – the last of the holidays – were among the happiest that Sally had ever known. Not only did she really begin to grow up, without realizing it, but she learned that there is nothing in the world which can take the place of good friends. Suddenly the Richardsons found themselves almost embarrassed by the kindness and friendship of the most unexpected people, and as soon as they knew that Margaret was getting well so quickly that she would be home soon an excitement, perhaps of thankfulness and relief, seized them all so that they said and did the craziest things.

Each day something different and unexpected happened and there was so much to do that Paul once said, 'What's so peculiar about all this is that it wouldn't have happened if Mother hadn't been ill.'

Phelpy, of course, proved a wonderful friend, but she was now almost accepted as one of the family. Then, when the Langtons came home and heard the news, Mrs Langton, vague but charming as usual, invited all the Richardsons to stay with them, while the vicar told Wilfred that he would take him over to the hospital at any time in his car. Mr Quirk sent round a box containing three tablets of expensive soap to Margaret with his compliments. Mrs Brand, whom they hardly knew, rang up Sally one morning and told her not to worry about lunch as Jimmy would be bringing them over a cooked steak-and-kidney pudding at one o'clock. Major Knight brought flowers from his garden and so did the milkman. John Wilkins brought Veronica over in the car almost every day and plenty of farm produce as well, and Wilfred admitted with a smile that business was better because so many people came into the *Wise Owl* to inquire after his wife.

Then there were the visiting days at the hospital when the vicar took them all – including Veronica, who came home at the end of the first week – over in his car and they saw Margaret looking young and pretty sitting up in bed surrounded with flowers and fruit and books.

Tony went back to London on the Wednesday, after all. Wilfred told him that he should and so, as it was early-closing day, they all went to the station to see him off. When the train came in old Ernest, the porter, found him a carriage and put his cases on the rack. Wilfred shook hands with his nephew and suddenly the children were smitten with an idiotic shyness. Tony was leaning from the window grinning sheepishly, with the puppy under one arm, when Sally suddenly leaned forward, put her hands on the edge of the open window and, on tiptoe, said, 'Come back to the Furnace Fête, Tony. It won't be the same without you.'

The whistle blew, the train moved off, and Tony was still waving when the last coach had rounded the curve.

Paul rammed his hands in his pockets and gave his sister an amused grimace.

'We've had a lot of fun with Tony after all,' he grinned. 'It would be wonderful for him to have a sister like I have.'

Elizabeth came round on the morning after her return

and although it was not possible to have an official meeting of the Owlers as Sally was busy in the house, Paul went over to fetch Jimmy and they unfolded their plans for the fête while Sally, in her mother's apron, was at the kitchen sink.

'You'll have to manage mostly without me, Liza,' she said. 'I've got to look after Dad but there ought to be lots you can do. We've fixed it all up with Major Knight and you can go and see him if you're not sure, and I expect he's arranged everything with your father by now . . . I should think you ought to ask Charles to help you, even if he's not an Owler.'

'That's all very well,' Elizabeth said, 'and it's true that I don't suppose we can do everything by ourselves although we know how efficient Jimmy is, but if we ask Charles before we've made up our minds he'll organize everything and it won't be our show at all. Let's ask him *after* we've made up our minds and not before.'

Paul fetched the grubby notebook in which they had entered their ideas and they finally fixed their plans while Sally, with Elizabeth's help, was trying to cook some buns and Paul made some tea. They decided first to call their effort the 'Junior Furnace Fête', and to have these words lettered on a banner which would be suspended over the entrance. There was some argument as to whether they should charge extra for admission to their corner but eventually they decided that their efforts would be worth an extra sixpence of anybody's money, and it was left for Jimmy to arrange for the lettering and fixing of the banner, while Veronica was to be responsible for the admission tickets which were to be inscribed in water colours or crayons – 'J.F.F. Admit One. 6d.' Actually Veronica tackled this so ably that there seemed to be a danger of her tongue protruding permanently from one corner of her mouth. During the last few days when the demand for tickets was brisk the words 'Admit One' danced before her eyes wherever she looked.

They also decided that their main effort was to be a stall at which they would sell anything and everything for children which they would collect during the time left to them.

'A stall like that is called a "White Elephant",' Liza explained, 'but let's call ours "The Junior Bazaar". I expect the grown-ups will have one but they're sure to charge a lot of money for their things so nothing on our stall should cost more than a shilling, and let's try and collect things people like us – children I mean – would like. We've all got something we can put in the bazaar and I bet there's a lot of things we shall want that other people have got.'

This suggestion was not at first received with wild enthusiasm, but if Paul was thinking of his 'relics' he didn't mention them.

'All right,' Sally agreed as she wiped some flour from her nose. 'You'll have to do most of the work but of course we ought to go to every house in the town and ask for jigsaws and books and toys and games .... Yes, Liza, it is a good idea. When we talked about it we only thought of the ordinary rubbish you see on most White Elephants . . . Who's going to go collecting?'

'Jimmy and me could do that,' Paul said. 'We'll have to make trucks that we can haul round behind our bikes

... That's O.K. ... That's something we could do. Where shall we store everything?'

'We've got an old shed behind the garage,' Liza explained. 'I'll tell Dad we want that. Did you get any more ideas without me?'

'I should say we did,' Jimmy burst out. 'Paul an' me are going to put on a two-man show. We'll build up a stage in the corner and while you're selling things at the bazaar we'll do our stuff ... Let me just tell you girls that we got a book with jokes and cross-talk and we're going to learn this up and I'll do *Laguna* and Paul's going to accompany me on that bazooka thing I got and we'll both black our faces —'

'I'm glad you're going to do that,' Elizabeth said, 'except, of course, that if you want to be really funny you just want to look yourselves,' at which Paul picked up one of Sally's uncooked buns and silenced her with it.

When order was restored Sally looked again at the notebook.

'We thought we'd get Vee to sell posies. You know what she is, Liza? Everybody, just like your father does, will say, "Isn't she a poppet?" and buy a bunch of flowers from her. We'll find her a baby sun-bonnet and she can carry the posies on a tray ... Maybe Hugh could do it, too?'

'That's one thing he wouldn't do. We could dress him up, though, and make him stand just outside our entrance and bang a drum. He'd like that and I think he'd make quite a stir ... And talking about a stir,' she added thoughtfully, 'oughtn't we to make and sell something to eat?'

The boys received this suggestion in stony silence.

'Scotch pancakes?' Elizabeth went on brightly. 'Don't you remember how Phelpy loved them? I can make them. Honestly I can, Paul. I could carry a tray of them round on my head and ring a bell.'

'You're mad,' Paul said. 'You're crazy, Liza. Something peculiar has happened to you. It's crazy enough to suggest that you try and sell something you've cooked, but why carry them on your head even if it will bear the weight, and why ring a bell?'

Elizabeth grimaced hideously at him.

'You're so ignorant, Paul, I'd be ashamed to open my mouth when intelligent people are present. If you'd ever read anything you would know that at the beginning of this century particularly, and sometimes now in London, men in green baize aprons used to walk the streets of big towns in the winter afternoons with a tray of muffins and crumpets balanced on their heads. So that people would know they were there they used to ring a bell . . . I think that if I pretended to be a muffin man with my Scotch pancakes we'd make some money and it would be a, a – a —'

'A bright idea?' Jimmy suggested helpfully.

'No. That's not the word although it is a bright idea.'

'Inner something?' Sally said.

'Innovation,' came triumphantly from Liza. 'You're an ignorant crowd – except Sall.'

'Keep your fingers out of the sultanas, Paul,' Sally went on. 'I had another idea, too, I saw a book in the shop – an old herbal book – and there were some ideas in it for making little bags of dried rose-leaves. I thought I could make some and we could sell those.'

'What do they do with 'em when they've got 'em? The mugs who buy them, I mean,' Jimmy asked with brutal logic.

'They smell them. In the book it's called "A Bag to Smell Unto' . . . Half a sec., and I'll go and fetch it.'

She whipped off her apron and dashed down to the shop.

'It's awful how quickly time goes,' she puffed as she came up three minutes later with the book under her arm. 'Dad says he'll be up in three-quarters of an hour so you'll have to go and buy a lettuce and some tomatoes, Paul, and we'll have corned beef – if there is any . . . Now look. Here it is. We'll ask Mr Quirk to give us mint and the cloves for the cause, and we'll get some bits of stuff to make the bags —'

'Who's going to make the bags?' Liza asked. 'Not me.'

'I'll ask Phelpy or Miss Mabel,' Sally said, 'and I'd like to tie a little label to each bag with the last bit printed on it . . . Read it, Liza. It's good.'

And this is what they read.

A BAG TO SMELL UNTO, OR TO CAUSE ONE TO SLEEP.

Take drie Rose leaves, keep them close in a glasse which will keep them sweet, then take powder of Mints, powder of Cloves in a grosse powder. Put the same to the Rose leaves, then put all these together in a bag, and take that to bed with you, and it will cause you to sleepe, and it is good to smell unto at other times.

'Shucks!' Paul whistled. 'And would people buy that to take to bed?'

These schemes proved to be quite enough in the hectic days which followed, for the idea of a Junior Fête soon caught on in Nettleford and the pile of toys and games in the shed behind the vicarage grew to remarkable proportions. Jimmy and Paul, with wheeled wooden boxes behind their bicycles, toured every road in the town, and wherever they called they tried to sell one of Veronica's 'Admit One' tickets, and in many cases were successful. And as they trundled to and from the vicarage with what Paul called their 'loot', you could see their lips moving silently and sometimes overhear an astonishing interchange of sentences as they learned their parts for the great act. At the vicarage, Elizabeth's brother Charles, at first with an air of condescension and later with enthusiasm, sorted out the loot and priced it with sticky tickets, and when he wasn't doing this he was helping in the field with the awning over the stall and the building of the stage for Jimmy and Paul's performance.

As soon as Veronica came back to the *Wise Owl* she was able to help Sally with the shopping when she wasn't doing 'Admit One's', but the latter was here, there and everywhere. Phelpy was wonderful, and when the cooking became too complicated she would come upstairs herself and take over while Sally went down to help her father. And every day there was good news from the hospital and on the second Wednesday, when the whole family went over in the vicar's car to see Margaret, she told them proudly that she was coming home on the Saturday.

'We'd better make a side-show of you, Mum,' Paul said. 'P'raps we could bring you straight to the fête and sit you in a special tent and charge for admission.'

'I'll try not to interfere with you at all, darlings. Daddy will come and fetch me so that you can get straight on with the show . . . Tell me some more.'

The great day dawned with rain. When Sally looked out of her window in horror the sky was filled with sullen clouds and the gutters were gurgling and singing as if they had never done anything else.

'It won't rain all day,' Wilfred said at breakfast. 'I heard the weather forecast. I'm going to close the *Wise Owl* this afternoon as everyone will be at the fête and I want Miss Phelps to go. She says she's going to take her sister in her chair and I'm going to hire a car and fetch your mother at three o'clock. I don't want you to fuss her and there's no need for any of you to come home until the evening. This is your show and we want you to enjoy it, so don't worry about us. Your mother and I have been alone together before now and we shall like it'. . . Another thing, Sally. We'll none of us have lunch here as we'll all be too busy. We'll go to the *Hobby Horse* and that will save time and trouble.'

As soon as he'd gone they flung themselves at the ordinary chores.

'There's something we've forgotten,' Sally said. 'Flowers for Mummy's bedroom, and if we could get a long strip of brown paper from the shop Vee can print "WELCOME HOME" on it . . . Couldn't you, Vee?'

'Yes, I could. Do I put "Admit One"? I hope not. But don't you all forget I got to get all my posies ready. I s'pose you know Aunt Mary is bringing me lots?'

Then Wilfred came upstairs.

'Telephone message for you,' he smiled. 'Tony is coming and bringing his mother too. Janet says she's going to stay and keep house for us until your mother is ready to take over. I suppose we can fit Tony in for a few days until he goes back to school? Janet says she's going to stay at the *Horse and Groom* to save us trouble. I must say that this is very handsome and unexpected of her. I'm sure your mother will be pleased.'

'That's O.K.,' Paul remarked. 'And the sun's out.' The morning passed in a flash.

The fête field was wet underfoot and steaming in the sunshine. There was a big tent for a flower show, some side-shows and several stalls for needlework, household goods, second-hand books and magazines and fruit and vegetables, but their own corner looked magnificent with its banner, and a gay, striped awning over the toy-stall and one to match it over the little stage. Charles and Sally set out the toys while Paul and Jimmy had a rehearsal in a corner of the vicarage garden. Elizabeth was cooking her Scotch pancakes and Veronica busy about the collection of her posies which children and people in all parts of the town had promised her.

The Richardsons met for lunch at the *Hobby Horse* and Wilfred came back to the vicarage field with them for the opening at half-past two before going off to fetch Margaret.

The sun was shining brightly now and the people of Nettleford crowded into the show. Little Hugh Langton beat his drum at the entrance of the Junior Furnace Fête, while his brother Charles stood behind a table with his father's top-hat on the back of his head yelling, 'Walk up, ladies and gents. Walk up!' Many of the people who came in with one of Veronica's 'Admit One' paid another sixpence and said it was a pleasure. To and fro among the crowd went Elizabeth, ringing her bell, but although she just could not balance her tray on her head she sold her pancakes well and was soon free to help Sally on the stall. Veronica in her party frock and sun-bonnet was a great success, but nothing compared with the turn put on by Jimmy and Paul. Mr Brand had fitted Paul with a suit identical with Jimmy's, and as the two boys were the same height the effect was excellent. They had also prepared several posters on brown paper which were displayed in prominent positions outside and inside the field.

DON'T MISS THE
NEW SMASH HIT
AT
JUNIOR FURNACE FÊTE

RASTUS AND
BONES
the
Coloured Coons
Give their famous Act at
3.30, 5.30, 6.30, 7.30,
and 8.30.

Silver Collection
for the Furnace.

WALK UP ! ! ! WALK UP

and promptly at quarter-past three Charles, with a megaphone, announced that Rastus and Bones were about to perform. Paul, of course, was not nearly so comfortable as Jimmy when they came on to the stage and set down two stools, particularly when he noticed Tony and his mother coming into the enclosure. Jimmy opened the show by singing *Lily of Laguna*, accompanied by his partner, and then the two coons settled down to their cross-talk, which was not always easy to follow as they laughed uproariously at their own jokes. Most of their quips started, 'Rastus (or Bones) can you tell me the difference between — ?' whereat Bones (or Rastus) would reply, 'Are you asking me what is the difference between — ?'

Perhaps the most successful of the coons' jokes was 'Bones, ma friend, can you tell me what it is that has four wheels and flies?'

'You are asking me, Rastus, what is it that has four wheels and flies . . . Tell me, Rastus, what it is that has four wheels and flies?'

'I'll tell you, Bones, what it is, etc. It's a dustcart, Bones!'

And after that they sang *Swanee River* together and then *Old Man River*, in which a young man in the audience joined with enthusiasm, and then Jimmy played them out with *Laguna* again while Charles stood invitingly at the entrance with an old hat, and by six o'clock everybody at the fête was humming and whistling the same lilting melody.

Between their turns the two performers stood in their make-up at the entrance inviting people to come in, while Charles made repeated journeys to the secretary's tent where Major Knight polished his eye-glass each time as he counted the money. 'Wonderful, my boy. The success of the show. Knew you youngsters would carry it off . . . Come and look at these figures, Vicar . . . You'll be able to buy two furnaces if they go on like this.'

Aunt Janet, who was very friendly, told Sally early in the afternoon that she had been to the *Wise Owl* and that her mother was safely home in bed and looking very well and had sent a message to say that none of them was to come until the fireworks were over. As soon as Veronica had sold the last of her posies she attached herself to Tony until she saw Phelpy with her sister in her wheeled chair.

The hours sped by until Sally and Elizabeth hated the sight of the toys and games left on their stall. They had said 'Good afternoon' and 'Hullo' so many times that their voices were hoarse, their feet ached, their hands and faces were sticky and their frocks grubby. The air smelled of crushed grass and people, and when there was a lull in the chatter they could hear the rooks cawing in the elms in the corner of the field.

'They sound like some of the people we've had this afternoon,' Liza said. 'Do you remember the woman who said she didn't want that Snakes and Ladders because the snakes' faces were cruel? You know the one, Sall. The woman with the jutting out front in a black hat . . . What's this parcel under the table?'

'Oh, Liza. It's my "Bags to Smell Unto". I've forgotten them. We'll have to sell them now.'

'How many are there?'

'Twenty. I thought we'd charge a shilling each.'

'So we could. Let's put them on the counter.'

Then the Major came up and glared through his eye-glass at them, although his stare was really very friendly.

'Wonderful, Sally . . . Congratulations to all. Amazed at those two boys . . . What's all this? Something still unsold?'

Sally explained.

'How much? One shilling each. Here you are, my dear. Buy the lot . . . Hear your mother is safely home. Take her these bags with my best wishes . . . Insist . . . Please don't argue . . . Goodbye, my dears,' and then quite unexpectedly, 'God bless you both.'

'Well!' Elizabeth gasped. 'I think he's an old pet.'

'Liza. I've got an idea. Do something for me? I want to go home now. Will you look after the stall and there's no need to tell the others. I must go and see Mother and I'll come back if I can. Vee is with Aunt Janet, I think. She'll be all right for a bit . . . Will you, Liza? Thanks awfully.'

She slipped through the crowd, dodged Aunt Janet, Tony and Veronica at one of the side-shows, and ran up the almost deserted High Street and then down the little court to their back door.

Across the doorway of their parents' bedroom was the banner, 'Welcome Home', and there was Margaret sitting up in bed, looking paler than usual, with Wilfred at her side.

'I told you not to come, darling,' she said. 'But I'm very glad to see you . . . Daddy and I have been enjoying ourselves and, oh, Sall, it is so wonderful to be home . . . What are all those lovely little bags?'

Sally explained about her own work and of Major Knight's kindness, and then went over and kissed the top of her father's head and leaned out of the window. The sky was a clear, dark blue as the dusk came slipping down. The first bright star showed above the distant elm trees and in the silence they could hear the murmur of the crowds in the fête meadow. There was a smell of warm earth, roses on the wall below and even of the 'Bags to Smell Unto' on her mother's bed.

And as she leaned out, feeling a glow of tired happiness which she could not possibly explain, the first firework shot up into the darkening sky, burst with a crack and threw out a train of coloured fire.

'You can't see the fireworks from there, Mummy,' she said. 'I'll explain them to you, if you like.'

'But wouldn't you like to run back to the others? It will all be over in half an hour, surely, and I shall still be here. I'm never going away again.'

'No thanks. I'd rather stay . . . The loveliest, most wonderful day of all my life has nearly gone . . . Not just because you've come home, and not just because of the fête, but because I've never known a day when everybody has been so nice . . . Aunt Janet was nice too, and I never liked her before.'

Three more fireworks whooshed upwards and Sally turned from the window and went on, 'Now it's nearly over and there'll never be another day like it.'

Her mother laughed – not quite so boisterously as usual – but with so much sympathy.

'I know, Sall. I've often felt like that. But tomorrow is another day waiting for us all to make the best of here, in our own home, and I'm not even going to begin to spoil you all by telling you how much I've missed you.'